Invasion of the Ninja

Book One of the Adventure Chronicles

Jeffrey Allen Davis

GCD Publishing
St. Charles, MO

GCD Entertainment
St. Charles, MO

ISBN-13: 978-0615628363
ISBN-10: 0615628362
Invasion of the Ninja: Book One of the Adventure Chronicles

Unless otherwise noted, all Bible verses are quoted from the King James Version (KJV) of the Bible.

Published by GCD Publishing
Visit us online at: www.gcdpublishing.tk
Text Set in Georgia
Printed and bound in the USA
Cover Art by Jason Richardson
Edited by Karen Griffiths
Additional Proofreading by Rob Gevjan

To my mom, Patricia Ann Davis, who taught me that a hug is the best medicine for whatever afflicts me.

“Be not overcome of evil, but overcome evil with good.”-Romans 12:21

Acknowledgements

Thanks to Jesus, my Blessed Savior.

Thanks to Karen Griffiths, my editor.

Thanks to Rob Gevjan for being an awesome proofreader.

Thanks to Darryl Sloan for all of his advice.

Thanks to Uncle Donald and my buddy, Michael Burlison, for putting up with my incessant questions about guns.

Thanks to my mother, whose heart knows no bounds.

Thanks to my hard-working father, who has already gone Home.

Thanks to my beautiful wife, Vickie, for her support during the long hours of writing. Thanks to my daughter, KK, for the calming effects of her hugs. Thanks to my stepson, Jay, for reading–and enjoying—the original version of this book. Thanks to my stepdaughter, Bree, for reminding me that I have to laugh every once in a while.

Thanks to D. Issac, B. Goodman, E. Griffiths, T. Thompson, D. Middleton, S. Black, J. Don Davis, L. Isaac, K. Corbett, E. Hall, J. Hall, L. Ringstaff, J. King, J. Decker, D. Goodman. You've all been lifelong influences.

About the Author

In 1989, when Jeffrey Allen Davis was fourteen, he started a recording on his parents' VCR to get a horror movie about a Ouija board. It captured the movie that came on Showtime after it, as well. That accidental recording, a ninja movie that starred Michael Dudikoff, grabbed his imagination and the shadow warriors have been hiding there ever since. Over twenty years later, he still enjoys watching a good ninja movie.

Davis lives in St. Charles, MO, with his wife, Vickie, his daughter, Kaitlyn, and two stepchildren, Jayson and Breeanna.

Visit him online at www.jeffreyallendavis.angelfire.com and his blog, jeffreyallendavis.wordpress.com.

Invasion of the Ninja

THE WAR

In the year 1530, AD, a conflict rose between the peaceful Funakoshi ninja clan and the war-like Waruiyatusu clan. A wedding . . . or, rather, the lack of one . . . caused the war. The *jonin*, or leader, of the Waruiyatsu, a cold-hearted man named Kondo, asked for the hand of the loveliest of the Funakoshi *kunoichi*, or female ninja, in marriage. Mitsu, Kondo's intended bride, was the daughter of the Funakoshi jonin, Koji, who reasoned that the marriage would form an alliance between the two clans. His intention was to give his blessing.

Until the two jonin discovered her in the arms of another man.

Enraged, Kondo accused Koji of attempting to disgrace him. The Warui leader issued a challenge to the Funakoshi leader and the two warriors met on the battlefield, violently wounding each other. They both died, no clear winner settling the question of honor. At this, Kondo's eldest son ordered an attack and the resulting battle saturated the ground with blood as ninja after ninja fell, defending what he believed to be the honor of his clan. Both sides retreated from the field that day.

The members of the elder council of the Funakoshi clan felt that blood was more important than gender and declared that Mitsu would take her father's place as the new jonin. Some of the individual families in the clan were angered to have a woman as their leader, but she proved herself time and time again as the war continued for the next thirty years.

When she was killed in battle, she was celebrated as one of the greatest of the Funakoshi leaders.

Over the centuries, the Warui ninja have retained their traditional ways, living within their own village in the mountains of Japan, from which they would send assassins to kill the Funakoshi, who have tried their best to advance with the times. The latter clan, whose members still remain close in their loyalties to one another, has moved into society, trying to cope with an ancient and relentless enemy.

Now, in the late 1900s, two young members of the Funakoshi and their friends are going to be forced to take up arms once again to continue an ancient war . . ..

Prologue
November 16, 1991
Friday, 6:30 AM

The bridge bustled with activity this morning. Its old, steel supports were rusted and weary, and it was time to remove and replace them. The crew worked well together and the foreman figured that this should be an easy job.

Sera was a small town. Everybody knew everybody else. The town consisted of about eight hundred people, with the graduating high school class averaging forty students. The geography of the town was what made it unique. The Current River ran across the western city limit, while an unnamed creek ran across the eastern. The bridges that crossed these two moving bodies of water were the only ways into or out of town. The bridges spanned the river and the large creek, which made its bustling tourist trade possible. While Will, the crew's foreman, considered this job no different than any other, the mayor had considered it a top priority.

Will, watching the crane from the safety of the bank of the creek, chuckled at the memory of the stern speech given at the town council meeting last week. "You know how important it is for you guys to have this job done before the parks open this summer, right?" he had demanded.

Duh.

Will had stopped him cold by bragging that his crew could finish it in less than a month, rather than the four months that they had been allotted. It was still nice to think about how he had stolen the words of the old pencil-pusher.

A large splash in the water caught his attention and he glanced in the direction of the flowing creek. “What happened?” he called out to Paul, the driver of the crane.

The latter had been climbing into his seat and had been facing the water. “Looks like Mike fell off the bridge!” Paul yelled back.

Will exhaled, blowing mist into the air. The water was probably freezing. He swore. “Is he okay? I don’t need any of you catching pneumonia!”

Another crewman yelled from farther up the bank of the creek, “He’s not moving!” Will pulled his safety hat off and threw it to the ground, breaking into a run toward the water. He dove in. The icy liquid hit him like a fist, knocking the wind from him as he swam for his fallen worker.

Finally, he reached Mike, who floated, face-down, twenty feet off shore. “Mike?” asked Will from between breaths. “Are you okay?” He spun him over.

A four-pronged, metal star protruded from his friend’s eye. Horrified, Will pushed the body away from him with a screech.

Screams and shouts erupted from the worksite. Will looked toward the shore to see the crane swing wildly. Paul sat in the driver’s seat, his blood-soaked jacket plastered to his chest. He saw a figure, clad head-to-toe in black, leap from the vehicle. The crimson-covered blade of his short sword glistened in his hand.

Arrows rained down from other figures, who had perched in the supports under the bridge. Each one was dressed identically and each arrow hit true.

Will watched, his heart pounding in his chest, as his men were slaughtered.

Panic filled the man as he swam for the other side of the creek, not caring that he had just released the contents of his bowels in the creek. He had to get away. He had to get out of sight of the grotesque scene.

He climbed out onto the bank closest to the town. He only had thirty feet to run to reach the safety of the trees.

Fear allowed him to forget the cold numbness that washed over his body from the frigid water. Fear allowed him to forget the dragging weight of his soaked and soiled clothing. He rushed for the trees.

Twenty feet.

Fifteen feet.

Ten feet.

I'm gonna make it!

Then a black-clad figure dropped from the front tree. Hanging upside down, its blade glinted in the sunlight as it slashed across Will's neck. Will felt a sharp, agonizing pain shoot across his throat. Then a warm sensation washed down the front of his body. For an instant, his befogged mind welcomed the warmth as it fought off the cold of the air against his wet chest.

Then he realized that the warmth was from his own blood. Gasping for air, his bulging eyes focusing on the person who had just killed him, he dropped to the ground as the darkness claimed him.

* * *

As the last of the bodies were piled under a huge tarp, one of the black-clothed figures walked up to another. “He lives on the rural side of this bridge, Master?”

The other figure looked out over the creek, seeming to see something that the other could not. “He does.” He clasped his hands together, finger through finger, with the two index fingers flat against each other and pointing straight up. “But that is not all.” He looked at the younger man, one of his clan’s *chunin*, or lieutenants, and continued. “She and her uncle, the *jonin*, live in that direction, as well. If we play this correctly, we may be able to wipe out the Funakoshi’s leadership in one, great sweep.”

The chunin bowed respectfully to his master and walked away. The ninja leader continued to stare out toward the rural area to the east of the small Missouri town. “Tonight we will have our vengeance, Funakoshi.”

Chapter One
November 16, 1991
Friday, 3:00 PM

The adolescent fixed his blue eyes upon the clock that hung above the chalkboard. *Five minutes.* He sighed and looked around the room, taking in everything from behind his glasses. Tim Brown, the teacher, sat at his desk, grading the tests that the students had just turned in. Amy Weston, the raven-haired beauty who could have any boy she wanted, sat near the windows, surrounded by adoring boys. In the back of the room, John Bowers, the captain of the basketball team, kept the rest of the class entertained by pointing their attention to Freddy Jenks, his lackey. Freddy tilted his head back and emptied an entire can of squirt-cheese into his mouth. The guys who watched cheered.

Jamie sighed and looked back at the clock. Two minutes had passed.

"Lookin' forward to this weekend?" asked George Tanner, Jamie's friend, from his place in the next seat.

Jamie nodded. "I haven't seen my friends from Jameston in nearly a year."

"Any chance of getting an invite out there?"

Jamie nodded. "I think that can be arranged." He looked back up at the clock, frustrated by the agonizing slowness of time. "I thought you were going to the dance tonight."

"I am," replied George. "Since my mom's helping Mr. and Mrs. Brown chaperone, she wouldn't let me stay home."

Jamie chuckled. "Sorry."

George grabbed his backpack from the floor and stuffed his textbook inside. "Not half as sorry as I am. I don't like a lot of people. But I could come out tomorrow."

A crumpled piece of paper sailed through the air and struck George in the back of his curly, blonde-covered head. The two teens turned to see John and Freddy looking at them with a smirk. Freddy, cheese running disgustingly down his chin, held both hands up, an obscene gesture on each.

Then his face lost its smirk when Mr. Brown called out from his desk, "Freddy, go to the bathroom and wash that stuff off! Act your age for once!"

Freddy climbed from his seat and walked to the door of the room, passing between Jamie and George as he did so. He smelled of cigarette smoke mixed with the odor of the cheese.

As Freddy reached the door, Mr. Brown asked, "Did your parents do a lot of drugs in the Sixties?"

George and Jamie burst out laughing, followed by Amy and the boys who sat around her.

Freddy glared at Jamie as he walked out the door. But he said nothing under the stern gaze of the teacher. While Mr. Brown was respected, having been declared Favorite Teacher in the yearbook all four years that he had been in this school, the students knew better than to push their luck with him.

The bell signaled the end of classes for the week. Jamie leaped to his feet.

“Why are you in such a hurry?” demanded George. “You can’t move any faster than the bus you’ll be on.”

Jamie sighed. George was right. Jamie should have gotten his license last year, but the town had been using the country road that led to his house to store a mound of gravel for fixing other roads in the area. Since there was only one open lane, Jamie had felt uncomfortable practicing over the summer. Of course, he realized that this was a rather pathetic excuse. Perhaps he was just too scared to take the test.

As they headed out of the room, Jamie said, “I hope you can make it tomorrow. My dad’s going to try to barbecue.”

“Won’t the smoke bother his emphysema?”

“That’s why I said *try*. If he doesn’t finish, Mom’ll probably do it . . . that is, if she can pry the barbecue fork from Buster’s hands.”

Jamie’s Sera friends had actually met Jamie’s Jameston friend, Buster, as well as Jamie’s cousin Zack. Buster was going to college next year to prepare for the ministry. Zack, on the other hand, was constantly hitting on girls, with varying degrees of success.

“Buster’s going to be there?” asked George as they walked by the science room. The pungent smell of formaldehyde filled their nostrils.

“Yep.” Jamie waved at Mr. Freedman, the short, balding science teacher, who was in the room cleaning up a spill. “Zack, too.”

“Zack?” George groaned. “Maybe I’ll pass on comin’ out after all.”

"Don't worry," chuckled Jamie. "My friend, Yoshi, is going to be there. She can usually keep him in line."

"Are they dating?"

Jamie looked at his friend and cocked one eyebrow. "No, and, if you value your life, I wouldn't ever ask *her* that."

"Oh, tough girl, huh?"

"You could say that."

The two stopped in front of their lockers and began putting their books away. Suddenly, George glanced behind Jamie and his eyes widened. This and the putrid smell of cheese breath mixed with cigarette smoke gave Jamie just enough warning to yank his hand out of his locker before the door slammed shut. The resounding metal **BANG** echoed through the hallway. Few of the other students paid attention, as such acts of bravado were common from Freddy Jenks.

"Thought that was funny, didya?" demanded Freddy, standing in front of John Bowers, who watched the confrontation with a smirk.

"What Mr. Brown said?" asked Jamie. "Hilarious."

"I'M GONNA BEAT THE DOG-MEAT OUTTA YOU!" growled Freddy as he reared back and swung his left fist, in a wide arc, straight toward Jamie's head.

Without thinking, the young man pulled his head back and out of the way, while grabbing the bully's moving wrist and using its own momentum to carry his fist painfully into the locker next to Jamie's.

Freddy grasped his hand and groaned in pain.

Uh oh, thought Jamie, *I'd better do something before I blow my cover*. Jamie quickly looked at the locker that Freddy had inadvertently punched, mustering as much of a look of surprise as he could. "Wow," he muttered, trying to sound shocked. He glanced at George, whose shock was genuine.

"Where'd you learn how to do that?" demanded John.

From a ninja master in Jameston, popped into Jamie's head. Two years of practice kept it from coming out of his mouth. Instead, he asked, "Do what?"

"What you just did to Freddy!"

Jamie shrugged. "It was just dumb luck, I guess."

John took a menacing step toward Jamie. "Then you won't mind me trying what he did."

"Is there a problem here, gentlemen?" asked a deep voice from behind John. Deck Pendragon, a curly-haired, red-bearded behemoth of a man, regarded the situation coldy.

Jamie sighed in relief. Deck, who was the substitute art teacher this week, was also a skilled weapons-maker. Since he had been the one commissioned to make Jamie's sword, he was the only person in Sera, outside of Jamie's family, who knew the teen's secret.

"Uh, no," responded John good-naturedly. "Nothing at all."

Deck folded his massive arms across his equally massive chest. "Let's keep it that way."

Suddenly, a girl's voice called out affectionately, "John!" Jamie looked past his antagonist to see Laura Blanton, Shawna Weston and her cousin, Amy Weston (the dark-haired girl in Jamie's last class), walking toward them. Laura was the one who had called out. It seemed like a yearly tradition that the head cheerleader and the head of the basketball team should date, and these two were no exception. However, the whole school knew of John's violent temper and the fact that he focused it on his lovely, blonde girlfriend. The only person with the guts to speak out against John was Laura's best friend, Shawna.

Shawna was a bit of a mystery. She was Jamie's class's projected valedictorian. However, there was a six-month period of time when Shawna had simply disappeared from the school the previous year. Jamie figured that, as her closest friends, Laura and Amy knew where she had been, but they weren't talking.

Laura approached John, taking his hand in hers, and kissed him gently on the lips.

Deck cleared his throat. "Public displays of affection can earn ya a detention."

Laura blushed. "Sorry, Mr. Pendragon."

"I'll let it slide this time."

Jamie sighed again and shook his head in bewilderment. How could she stay with him?

Jamie looked at Shawna and Amy. Shawna stared daggers at her friend's boyfriend.

John seemed to notice Shawna's distaste, as well. He grinned at the female honor student and asked, "Jealous?"

Shawna cocked an eyebrow and declared, "When your IQ gets out of the double-digits, call me."

Deck gave Jamie a knowing look, being the only person present who understood the control that

Jamie was maintaining. Then he turned and walked away.

John put his right arm around Laura's waist. "Tell ya what," he said to Jamie with a glare. "I'm gonna let you off this time, since Mr. Dragonhead had to butt in. Just don't overstep your bounds again, geek. Remember, I'm everything here, and you're nothing." He put his arm around Laura's shoulders, leading her toward the building's front doors, followed by Freddy, who was still cradling his sore hand.

Jamie could hear Laura say, "That wasn't very nice, John."

The basketball star replied with, "Don't start with me, Laura . . ." and then their voices trailed off.

Shawna stepped up to Jamie and said, "You know what they say . . . if you give a bully one good slug, he'll leave you alone."

Jamie smiled shyly and ran his fingers through his light brown hair. He looked up. Shawna's shoulder-length hair was naturally dark, but she dyed it blonde. The eyes that peered out from behind her glasses were brown, but surprisingly bright. She was pretty, in a natural and sweet way. "Thanks for the tip," he responded.

"Are you going to be at the dance tonight?" asked Amy, ignoring the various boys in the hall who were staring longingly at her.

Jamie shook his head as he threw his backpack over his shoulder. "I'm having company up for the weekend." He shrugged. "Can't make it."

Shawna smiled at him. It left him slightly breathless. "Too bad. I was going to save you a dance."

Jamie cleared his throat. "Can I take a rain check?"

She reached out and gently touched the side of his arm. "Of course. There'll be plenty more dances before we graduate next year." Then she turned with Amy and headed toward the front exit.

George slapped his friend on the back. "Why don't you just ask her out?"

"Are you kidding?" returned the young ninja. "I don't think she has time to date, with all the studying she does."

"People like that don't need to study. They learn by osmosis."

As the two approached the front doors, George commented, "She was right, you know. You should just kick John and Freddy's . . .."

"I don't like to fight," interrupted Jamie.

George gave his friend a crooked smile. "That's because you don't know how to do it. If you learned, you'd have a lot more confidence."

Jamie chuckled inwardly at the irony. If George only knew.

* * *

The top floor of the school building was smaller than the ground floor. The second floor only had five rooms, so much of the building was only one story. The side of the building where the Home Economics room sat above the first floor's gym blocked the sun in the afternoon as school was being released for the day, leaving the center of the roof bathed in shadows. But today, one of those shadows was alive. It crept quietly to the edge of the roof, looking down at the students below.

Its eyes settled on two figures as they walked out of the school building and down the small hill that led to the bus-loading zone and parking lot. When they reached the latter, they said something to one another, then separated. One walked toward the student vehicles, and the other toward the end bus. The figure focused on the second boy. It was him who Master Obata wanted. Raleigh was one of the Funakoshi chunin, trained by their leader, Tanemura Funakoshi. The members of the Warui clan hated this teenage ninja even more than the other Funakoshi ninja. Unlike the natural members, who were born into the war, he had chosen his side. It was a choice that would cost him his life.

The figure retreated back into the shadows . . ..

* * *

Jamie sat next to his friend, Jeremy King, watching in fascination as Jeremy looked through a deck of cards. The dark-haired youth, who was two years younger than Jamie, examined each individual card, as if committing it to memory, before putting it back into the deck.

Jamie tried to control his breathing. As Jeremy lived with his parents in a cabin in the woods, with no running water or electricity, he tended to smell rather ripe by the weekend. Jamie sighed. People found ways to cover their scents before running water was invented. Why couldn't Jeremy?

Across the aisle, Steve Adams sat with his brother, Max. Steve, his blonde hair shaved into a crew cut, and Jeremy were in the same class in school and were best friends who shared a fascination with fantasy fiction. Steve's girlfriend, Leslie, sat in the seat in front of them. Steve and Leslie were competing for valedictorian of their class. Jeremy didn't seem to care, as long as his grades were good enough to graduate.

Max, who was normally the most hyper of the bunch, stared out of the window in boredom.

Jamie glanced toward Jeremy, sitting next to the window, and asked, "Is Deck going to be at the dance tonight?"

Jeremy looked at Jamie and, fishing through one of his many coat pockets, replied, "I think so. He was subbing for Mr. Jackson today in my art class. Said he'd be a little late. He's gonna put some new traps around his house first." The house that Jeremy was referring to was actually a miniature castle that Deck had build by hand, complete with working drawbridge.

"Yeah, I saw him in the hall after school," said Jamie. "He bailed me out of a conflict with John Bowers."

Steve's voice carried over the aisle. "I heard about what you did to Freddy's hand. How did you learn to do that?"

Jamie hoped that he was not going to have to answer that question many more times. "I don't know. Just dumb luck, I guess."

"Maybe you should come with me to my tae kwon do class," suggested Max, who was a red belt. "If you did it by accident, you may just be a natural."

A shirt went flying between Jamie and Jeremy, landing on the back of the seat in front of them. Troy

Shockley and Tray Peterson were goofing off again. They had an annoying habit of taking off articles of clothing and throwing them all over the bus. Jamie even remembered a time when Troy's underwear ended up on the bus-driver's head.

Jeremy looked at Jamie. "When are you gonna get your license so we don't hafta go through this every day?" He grabbed the shirt and nonchalantly tossed it out the window.

A few seconds later, Tray looked over the seat and asked, "Either'a you two geeks seen my shirt?"

Jeremy looked back at him and replied, "Yep."

After a few seconds of silence, Tray's eyes widened in annoyance as he realized that Jeremy was not going to elaborate. "Well, where is it?"

Jeremy looked back at them and smiled. "About a mile back."

"WHAT?!" exploded the eighth-grader. "It flew out the WINDOW?!"

Jeremy snapped his fingers in mock-defeatist style. "Wind took it."

"Oh, great! My mom's gonna kill me!" The eighth-grader plopped back in his seat and angrily folded his arms across his bare chest.

Jamie couldn't stop himself from chuckling.

Jeremy thrust out both hands, the cards fanned out. "Pick a card . . . any card."

Jamie cocked an eyebrow, guardedly pulling a card from the deck and looking at it. It was the eight of clubs. Jeremy placed his hand on his seatmate's head and began humming, as if in meditative concentration. Jamie could see Steve, Leslie and Max, just inside his field of vision, watching in fascination.

Now Jeremy opened his eyes and instructed, "Let me see your card." Jamie, his eyebrow still cocked, flipped the card over so that his eccentric young friend could see it. "Yep, that's what I thought it was." Jamie rolled his eyes. He knew that Jeremy was just being playful, but he sometimes could not help but wonder if the young man, who readily told people that he was the reincarnation of Robin Hood, wasn't really walking on the edge of insanity.

As the bus crossed the bridge that ran over the creek and city limit of Sera, Jamie noticed that the construction workers were still on the job. "I thought the bridge workers were only supposed to be working until three o'clock on Fridays."

Steve was reading an almanac. "Maybe they're trying to get a little ahead so that they don't have to come in as early on Monday."

Max, who had been unusually silent for over a minute, suddenly piped, "Hey, that one looks Asian!"

Jamie perked at this revelation and craned his neck, then climbed to his feet and leaned over Steve and Max's seat, trying to see this Eastern construction worker. Sure enough, there stood a man on the walkway of the bridge, his slightly slanted eyes showing his Japanese heritage.

The man looked curiously at the bus as it passed, then seemed to see Jamie behind Steve. As his eyes settled upon the teen, they narrowed and the young man felt a cold chill run up his spine. *Why did he look at me like that?*

"*There's* somthin' you don't see everyday," muttered Max as he regarded the man.

"Maybe he's related to that Yoshi-girl on the Aurthur quiz bowl team," suggested Jeremy. Jamie knew that this wasn't correct. He said nothing.

After the bus had passed the bridge, Jamie settled back into his seat. Steve got his attention. "Speaking of quiz bowl, tryouts are next week." He was looking right at Jamie.

"I know," replied Jamie. In the quiz show-like competition, all of the local schools competed. The teams were filled with the most intelligent students of the school; at least those who wanted to compete.

"Are you ready to try out yet?"

Jamie pushed his right hand up under his glasses, rubbing both eyes wearily. "I dunno."

"It's not like you're not intelligent enough," commented Steve.

"Well, I'm not exactly a straight-A student, either."

Steve closed the almanac, marking his place with his right index finger. "*Grades* have little to do with it." He gestured toward Jeremy. "He can barely keep his grades *acceptable*, but he's still on the team."

Jamie could hear Jeremy shift in the seat beside him as he chided, "Hey! I resemble that remark!"

Troy looked over the seat and said, "Yeah, a royal person doesn't need ta do good in school." Leaning halfway over the seat, he continued, "Oh, Jeremy King! Your *majesty*!" he said, feigning a bow.

Jeremy's eyes sparkled with humor. "Does this mean that you'll obey me?"

Troy performed that same mock bow. "*Command* me, lord!"

Jeremy puffed out his chest and demanded, "Remove all of your clothing, climb on top of the bus and wait for an eighteen-wheeler to come up behind us. Then jump off so that you land in its path, ending your miserable existence. THIS I COMMAND!!!"

Max chuckled. "You wouldn't have to command the first part. They like being naked." He gestured toward Troy's seatmate. "I mean, look at Tray. He threw his shirt out the window."

"Hey!" whined Troy's annoying friend. "I didn't throw it out the window! The wind took it!"

* * *

Jamie stepped off of the bus, looking across the road at the old house in which he and his parents lived with their cat, Linus, and Chihuahua, Chico. The adolescent was embarrassed to let his Jameston friends see this place again. The house was a total mess. The siding was falling off in places, leaving black patches of rotted fiberglass insulation all over the front of the house. The roof leaked in various places and the floor felt as if it could cave in at any moment.

Jamie sighed as he crossed the road in front of the stopped bus. As his feet crunched on the gravel on the side of the old pavement, the bus started to move slowly up the road. He could hear Tray and Troy whooping and hollering out of the window. He resisted the slight urge to copy Freddy's earlier obscene gesture and focused on the front door of his house as he approached.

The door had a footprint indented into the wood where one of his older brothers, Keith, had kicked open the door in a drunken stupor on one of his late-night visits because he could not wake anybody up to let him in.

As Jamie stepped onto the flat, concrete slab that served as the front porch, Linus met him. The grey and white-striped feline purred contentedly as he scratched him behind the ear. After unlocking the door, Jamie stepped inside, followed by his cat.

He closed the door and walked through the living room and into the hallway that separated the kitchen from his bedroom. He found Chico on his bedroom floor, having an asthma attack. After throwing the backpack on his bed, the young ninja picked Chico up from the floor and sat in the old easy chair that served as both his video game chair and his study chair. He gently held the shivering, old dog as it wheezed, looking up at him affectionately. Linus jumped into the chair and curiously sniffed the dog; neither was ever hostile toward the other.

Chico was something of a black sheep among the little Mexican dogs. Unlike the majority of the males that Jamie had ever seen in that breed, this little, snow-white one was not, as his mother would say, "a yipper." He was actually a very quiet old dog, unless his asthma was acting up. He actually belonged to Jamie's dad, Chuck, who himself had emphysema. The older man would often hold the little dog while both of them were having a breathing attack.

When Chico finally calmed, the teen leaned over to gently nudge the old dog's nose with his own, but the dog affectionately licked the boy's nose, instead. Jamie smiled and leaned his head back against the soft headrest of the chair.

He had almost blown his cover today. Had Deck not come along, he might have found himself having to fight John. And he had not wanted to reveal his past to even his closest friends in Sera . . ..

Chapter Two
Flashback
April 14, 1984
Saturday, 4:52 PM

The nine year-old boy nearly toppled as he turned his bike off of his home street of Speedway and onto the back street that connected all of the roadways that ran perpendicular to the cotton field. Rows of the local crop moved steadily by as Jamie steadied himself upon the two-wheeler. He was going to see his best friend, Buster.

The lad brought his bike to a stop, balancing on his right foot, as he noted a car up ahead that was parked on the side of the road, just past Polluck Street. The red sports car seemed out of place. Jamie had only seen a vehicle like it before while watching his favorite cartoon, "the Transformers." *Lamborghini*, realized the youth. *Wow!*

Standing next to the car, bent over and talking to someone through the front passenger's window, was a boy from school. He was a couple of years older than Jamie, and Jamie didn't know his name, but he knew that the boy was in Mrs. Stewart's sixth grade class.

As the boy stood up, an arm from inside of the car handed him something. With the curiosity of any child, Jamie pushed his glasses farther up on his nose and squinted his eyes to see the older boy's possession. It was a zip-top, plastic bag that contained white powder. The older boy gingerly opened the bag and stuck his finger lightly inside.

Pulling it out, he lightly touched his finger to his tongue. He smiled and nodded.

The realization hit Jamie all at once. Drugs. Jamie's eyes widened. The boy had just bought drugs. This shock turned to terror as the adolescent turned and looked directly at him.

"That kid saw us!" These words screeched into Jamie's ears as he shot down Polluck Street.

Why'd you have to stop and look, stupid?! he chided himself. Jamie had never known true fear until this very moment. His heart pounded in his chest and he gasped for breath as he heard the sound of the sports car coming up behind him.

Risking a look back, he saw, to his horror, that it was gaining fast. Rectangular headlights glared at him like the eyes of a hunting beast. The youth turned back around and put all of his strength into the pedals. His legs screamed in agony.

Realizing that the driver could run him over at any moment, Jamie swerved off of the road and into the yard of Tanemura Funakoshi, an old, Japanese man who had retired years ago to the small town. Mr. Funakoshi had always been kind to the neighborhood children. He would help Jamie.

The boy leaped from his bike as the Lamborghini, its driver caught off guard by Jamie's sudden turn, squealed to a stop in the street, Jamie ran up the front steps and pounded on the door. Putting his ear to the door, he heard nothing inside. He turned and glanced to the side to see the old man's Ford Taurus parked in the driveway. *He has to be home!*

Jamie was grabbed from behind and thrown off of the steps. He landed on grass with a painful *thud,* his nose striking the ground hard. Rough hands grasped him by the back of his blue *Spider-Man* T-shirt and turned him over to stare into the wild eyes of the boy who had bought the drugs. "My mom'n'dad'll kill me if they find out about this, ya hear?!" The older boy's hands searched out Jamie's throat and started constricting.

The younger boy punched at the older boy's sides in vain, his weak strikes barely even noticed by the crazed teen. The men from the car stood just inside Jamie's field of vision, laughing and throwing words of encouragement to his attacker. The young boy could not breathe. Flashes of light formed in his field of vision as his attacker began to slowly fade from view.

"Release the boy, NOW!!!" demanded a strong voice. As the sound of his own heartbeat echoed in his head and muffled anything outside, Jamie could not make out where the voice had originated.

Suddenly, the boy released him. Jamie reached up to rub his throat with both of his hands, coughing and gasping for breath. As his vision cleared, he could see why the boy had let him go. Standing at Jamie's right, a long, wooden staff in his right hand, was Mr. Funakoshi.

The older boy, now in a sitting position, was scurrying backward as fast as his hands and feet would take him. The two men started warily toward the Japanese man, each pulling a knife from his belt. Mr. Funakoshi spun the staff a few times between both hands. This seemed to make the two men even less sure of themselves.

"I do not know what has prompted this attack," he looked down at Jamie, who wiped his hand across his upper lip, eyeing the Japanese man in wonder, then looked back at the men, "but I will give you the option of leaving now without further confrontation."

One of the men lashed out with his knife, but Funakoshi had already moved to the side and slammed the shaft of the staff into the man's gut. As he doubled over, the Japanese man finished the fight with a well-placed strike to the back of the head.

Jamie focused upon Tanemura, as the old man assumed a defensive stance in preparation for an attack by the other man. Each step that the drug dealer took toward the older man seemed to echo through Jamie's head. In contrast, no sound seemed to be coming from Mr. Funakoshi at all.

The younger man lunged at the older. Tanemura's staff slammed into his opponent's hand, knocking the blade into the air. As it came back down, he swatted it and sent it flying across the yard to embed itself into a tree.

Tanemura dropped the staff to the ground. It came to rest in front of Jamie.

Jamie's eyes turned from the fight to look at the other boy. He had grabbed the knife from the unconscious man and was circling around the two combatants, trying to get behind the older man. Jamie looked around frantically. Reaching out with his right hand, he grasped the staff and climbed to his feet.

The boy had succeeded in getting behind Funakoshi, who gave no inclination that he knew that the boy was there. The boy held the knife under-handed, moving slowly toward the old man.

"HEY, JERK!" yelled Jamie. The boy turned to look at him as he swung the staff like a baseball bat, striking him across the face with it. The boy's head jerked to the side with the blow and he fell to the ground, unconscious. Then, the staff dropped from numb fingers and Jamie sunk back to the ground.

Tanemura continued defending himself against the final assailant. The old man blocked a clumsy punch to his face. Grabbing the man's wrist, Tanemura kicked him in the gut, then turned and flipped him to the ground. A final, open-handed strike the back of the man's head knocked him cold.

Jamie sighed with relief. Looking down at his hand, he noticed that there was a smear of red across it. He reached up and once again wiped it across his upper lip, then looked again. His nose was oozing blood. He must have busted it when the older boy slammed him to the ground.

The young boy looked back up at Mr. Funakoshi, who was fishing through the trunk of his car for something. He produced a long, black rope with a three-pronged hook at the end of it. Walking among the two men and the boy, he bound each one, hands and feet, connecting them to each other. He then searched each of them. Finally, he took the hooked end of the rope and tossed it toward one of the higher branches of the only tree in his front yard. The hook caught itself on the branch, anchoring the three thugs in place.

"That should hold them while I call the sheriff," commented the old man as he turned to look at Jamie with a smile. The smile faded as he focused on Jamie's face. "Your nose is bleeding. Come with me."

Jamie climbed unsteadily to his feet, his legs feeling like rubber. He moved slowly up the steps to the door and followed Tanemura inside. The living room drew its only light from the picture window in the front of the house. Mr. Funakoshi kicked off his shoes before he stepped off of the small tile entryway onto the carpet. Jamie did the same.

The man gently lifted Jamie's chin with his right hand and examined the boy's nose. "It doesn't appear to be very bad. Be seated while I get you a washcloth." He turned and headed down the hallway to the bathroom.

Jamie obediently walked across the room and sat on the couch, taking his glasses off and cleaning them on this shirt. After he put them back on, he examined the room. This was the first time that Jamie had been inside the house. Tanemura, a retired toymaker, would often entertain the neighborhood children with games and refreshments. But he always did this in his front yard.

The carpet was a light brown color. It looked brand new, which may have been Tanemura's reason for taking off his shoes. A large, console television stood in front of the picture window. On it was a strange-looking, potted tree. The branches grew out at odd angles. Jamie guessed it must be Japanese.

To his left, Jamie saw a rack on the wall that held two swords. One was a mirror image of the other, albeit smaller. Their handles were braided in black chord and the black sheathes slightly reflected the sunlight that streamed in the window.

To Jamie's right, his eyes settled on something that seemed out of place. It was a wooden cross. He did not take his eyes off of it when Tanemura walked back into the living room.

"I see that you found my cross," said the older man.

Jamie looked up at him and nodded.

"And you wonder why an old, Japanese man would have a cross in his living room?"

Jamie shrugged.

Mr. Funakoshi handed the washcloth to the boy as he replied, "I became a Christian when I came to America over thirty years ago. Now, Jesus is my Savior."

Jamie wiped the blood from his upper lip, then used the cloth to pinch his nostrils closed and tilted his head back.

"No, tilt your head forward," instructed Tanemura. "The bleeding will stop faster and you will not swallow more of your own blood."

Jamie did as he was told as Tanemura headed into the kitchen. He turned his head to watch as the old man grabbed the phone from its perch on the wall and dialed a number. The man waited for someone to answer on the other end. "Hello, Buster? May I speak with your father?"

That was to be expected. Buster's father was the police chief.

"Yes, Sheriff Goodman?" Mr. Funakoshi continued. "This is Tanemura Funakoshi. Some men attacked Jamie Raleigh in my front yard a few moments ago. I detained them and tied them up outside. Could you please come and collect them?" He waited as the sheriff said something. "Yes, assure Buster that Jamie is well. I was able to stop them before they did too much harm. I will see you when you arrive."

He hung up the receiver, then picked it back up and called out to Jamie, "What is your phone number?"

"Doo, four, sigs-doo, wad, four, seved," responded Jamie, his voice muffled with his nostrils pinched closed.

"Two, four, six-two, one, four, seven?"

Jamie nodded.

Tanemura dialed the number. "Mrs. Raleigh? This is Tanemura Funakoshi. I have your son in my house. There was a . . . situation and it would be good for you to come to my house." He waited for her reaction. "Yes, he is well. No, it was nothing that he did wrong." She said something. "We will await your arrival. If the men who are tied up in my front yard are conscious when you arrive, please do not approach them. I secured them as best I could but, if they get loose, they may still be dangerous." She said something else. "Yes, *they* were the ones who did something wrong." He hung up the phone.

Tanemura walked back into the living room and knelt before Jamie. "Let me see your nose."

Jamie removed the cloth and the old man examined him. "The bleeding seems to have stopped."

Jamie just stared at him.

"You are not very talkative, are you?"

The boy shrugged. "Only when I got somthin' important t'say."

Tanemura smiled. "Well, how about this? Perhaps you could tell me why those men were allowing that boy to attack you?"

"I saw'em sell him drugs," responded Jamie.

Tanemura's eyes narrowed. "Are you sure?"

"They gave him a bag with a white powder in it. When they saw that I saw it, they chased me."

The doorbell rang. As Buster's house was on the same street as Tanemura's, it had not taken the sheriff long to get there. Tanemura walked over to the door and opened it. Through the screen door, Jamie could see Mr. Goodman and a deputy handcuffing the men.

Buster stood on the porch.

Tanemura opened the screen door for Buster to enter. The youth did so as Tanemura called out, "You might wish to check the boy. Jamie said that they attacked him for seeing them sell the boy some kind of drug."

Buster ran up to Jamie. "Are you okay?"

Jamie nodded. "He saved me."

Tanemura nodded. "You did help a little. You dispatched the boy."

Buster's eyes widened in awe. "Wow! How'd you do that?"

"Hit'im upside the head with a bo staff," replied Jamie, swinging his arms for emphasis.

"How did you know that word?" asked Tanemura.

"Sho Kasugi," responded the youth.

"Who?"

"Sho Kasugi. He's in a bunch of movies about ninjas."

Mr. Funakoshi regarded Jamie thoughtfully. He looked across the room at the two swords. Then he focused on Jamie again. "Jamie, how would you like for me to teach you to defend yourself, as I did today?"

"Mom said we don't have the money for me to take lessons," was the boy's response.

"I would need your mother's permission, of course," returned Tanemura. "But I wouldn't charge you for the lessons. If your mother agrees, would you like to train with me?"

Jamie smiled. "Would you teach me karate?"

Tanemura chuckled. "Well, not exactly . . .."

Chapter Three
November 16, 1991
Friday, 4:47 PM

Jamie awoke with a start. He had dozed off while thinking of that day, so long ago. He had, indeed, trained under Tanemura Funakoshi. His sensei had trained him to be a ninja. He had worked hard, surpassing many of the other students of the various families in the clan. As he had put only his school work before his constant training, he had finished in just under five years.

It helped that his best friends from Jameston had followed his interest in the martial arts. While most of their peers were spending their time playing baseball during the summer, Jamie and his friends were sparring with each other.

Jamie looked down at Chico, sleeping contentedly on his lap. Linus lay on the right arm of the chair, his eyes barely open. He glanced at the metal footlocker at the foot of his bed. Once containing the *ninja-to* that Deck Pendragon had crafted for him, he had taken the sword and most of his other weapons to his sensei's house in Aurthur when Max had discovered his ninja suit in his closet. Convincing his younger friend that it was just a collectable had been easy, but the young ninja had not wanted to tempt fate again. Now, it only contained his practice sword, called a *bokken*, and his other practice weapons.

Jamie looked at the alarm clock at the head of his bed. He hadn't slept long.

The phone rang. Linus's ears perked up. Jamie leaned forward and grabbed the corded phone from the top of his television, ignoring Chico's whining protests, then answered it.

"Hello?"

The familiar voice on the other end had a slight accent. *"Jamie? It is Yoshi."*

He did not know why she announced herself. It's not like he had any other Japanese girls who called him regularly. "Hey."

"Have they arrived yet?"

"Not yet," replied Jamie with a yawn. "They should be here any time, though."

"I hope that Buster does not bring BJ."

Jamie shook his head. "Can you actually see Mrs. Goodman letting Buster go somewhere without dragging his brother with him?"

"Surely she must realize that a seventeen-year-old boy is too old to be taking his eight year-old brother with him everywhere. After all, what is she going to do when he goes to college next year?"

Jamie chuckled. "I hear that Evangel College has a daycare . . .."

"Not funny, Jamie Raleigh."

"Okay," he responded. "She'll have no excuse then but to take responsibility for her own kid."

He could hear her sigh. *"Are we still going to go to the skating rink?"*

Jamie cleared his throat. "If we have to."

"You know how much we all enjoy skating, particularly Dave."

"I know," said Jamie. "But I really tank at it."

"But we all know that you are capable of at least pretending *to have a good time,"* she laughed. *"And I will stay near you to help you if you fall."*

He smiled. "Thanks. I can walk a tightrope, but I'm a clutz on skates. Go figure."

"That, coupled with your fear of heights, makes you an interesting ninja, to be sure." She laughed again, then said, *"Call me when you are all leaving to pick me up."*

"Will do," he replied. "Bye, sis."

He heard the click on the other end.

After hanging up the phone, Jamie sat Chico gently on the floor. Then he stood and stretched. He called Yoshi "sis," as they were members of the same family within their clan. They had trained together, when she was taking it seriously, when they were younger. First, Jamie's sensei, who was Yoshi's great-uncle, would meet with her parents and the three of them would observe Jamie and Yoshi practice together. Then, after the death of Yoshi's parents, Tanemura had continued her training alone. By then, Jamie had completed his test of membership into the clan and spent as much time as possible helping in her training. It had been part of the reason Tanemura and Yoshi had followed Jamie West when his parents had moved their family to Sera. It had been highly important that Yoshi finish her training. She was the next in line to be the *jonin*, or leader, of their clan when Tanemura passed away.

A car horn blared from the front yard. Jamie rushed out of his bedroom and into the living room, looking out the window in the door to see his uncle, Donnie Isaac, climbing from the passenger's seat of a late model SUV. Jamie's cousin, Dave, climbed from the driver's seat.

Jamie opened the door and called out, "Your dad's actually letting you drive? He must be braver than I thought!"

Dave, who stood a good six inches taller than Jamie . . . but was six months younger . . . hollered back, "Nyuk, nyuk. Just call me when *you* get yer license." Dave reached back and absently checked the respectable ponytail into which he had tied his shoulder-length, brown hair.

Jamie smiled and folded his arms across his chest. "Fair enough."

Donnie walked around the SUV and, before climbing into the driver's seat, called out to Jamie, "I'm going to stay at that motel in Aurthur. Tell your mom I'll be by tomorrow."

"You're not going to stay here?" asked Jamie.

At that moment, a red, mid-eighties model minivan with a silver driver's side front door pulled into the driveway on the far side of Donnie's SUV. "I don't think there's going to be room," Jamie's uncle responded.

The silver door opened and Jamie's friend and nunchaku student stepped out. A year older than the young ninja, Buster stood just under an inch taller. His short, dark hair was disheveled by the wind that had been blowing in through his open window.

Jamie could hear an all too familiar voice yelling from within the van, "Get me outta here! I'm gonna barf!"

Buster slid open the side door and a short, pudgy child leapt out. The child bent at the waist and rested his hands on his knees, over-emphasizing the heaves.

"Are you okay, B.J.?" asked Buster in concern.

"He's fine," called out another voice from within the van . . . one that Jamie recognized as his cousin, Pete. "He's just suffering from 'lack of attention-itis.'"

"He really could be sick," commented Buster as he gently placed his hand on his brother's back.

"Yeah," called Jamie's other cousin, Zack, who was climbing out of the back passenger's door of Donnie's SUV, "we'll believe that when we believe you're a Satanist." He shook his head at his own sarcasm. This one, who was a year younger than Jamie, had fixed his short hair into a spike to match his favorite cartoon character, a rude child from a prime-time comedy series who was on the front of Zack's shirt.

Buster looked at Zack disapprovingly. As if to emphasize the irony of Zack's statement, Buster's silver cross fell into view from within his shirt, dangling from a thin chain around his neck.

Pete climbed from the van, throwing his backpack over his shoulder. "Of course," he said, running his fingers through his short, dishwater blonde hair, "with you drivin', it's a wonder we're not *both* hurling."

Buster cracked a crooked smile. "I didn't hear you complaining during the trip."

"Well, you still drive better than I could."

B.J. stood. "Okay, I'm better."

Dave rolled his eyes and grumbled, "This is gonna be a fun weekend."

Donnie started the vehicle. "You kids have fun. And watch the fighting, son."

Dave regarded his father in amusement. "Lemme get this straight. You want me t'have fun, but *not* fight?"

Donnie shook his head, then backed out of the driveway and drove back up the road.

Jamie stepped aside to allow his friends and cousins to enter. As B.J. stepped in, he noticed the damage to the front door. "What happened?"

"My brother kicked it," responded Jamie.

"Why?"

"Because he couldn't get anyone to let him in."

"Why?"

Jamie rolled his eyes. "Because it was three in the morning and everyone was asleep."

"Why was he coming home at three in the morning?"

Obviously noticing that Jamie was already getting annoyed, Buster interjected. "We're going skating tonight, B.J."

His brother glared at him. "Why didn't you tell me that when we were home so I could bring my skates?"

Buster shook his head. "They won't let you wear the *Fisher Price* skates at the rink."

"But I can't wear the ones they rent out," argued B.J.. "I'll get Athlete's Foot!"

"Oh, fer cryin' out loud, dude!" bellowed Dave. "Yer what . . . eight? Yer not gonna get *Athlete's Foot*! And they spray the shoes out with disinfecting spray after everybody wears'em!"

Jamie suppressed a chuckle. Like most of the older members of their fighting arts enthusiast club,

Dave did not like for Buster to have to drag his brother everywhere they went. Unlike the rest of them, he was not afraid to make it known.

"So, where's the skating rink?" asked Zack as he dropped the suitcase on the couch.

Jamie glanced at Zack. "The Bluff."

Pete sighed. "We just drove through there to get here. Can't we go in the opposite direction?"

Jamie shook his head. "There isn't anything in the opposite direction. Besides, it's out of our way if we're picking up Yoshi."

"So'd she finally finish her training?" asked Dave.

The young ninja nodded. "She took her test at the park at Water's Kiss in town, near the river."

"How'd she do?" asked Buster.

"She beat the stuffing out of us," laughed Jamie. "Give her two ninja-tos and she's absolutely amazing. She can match me on pretty much everything, but she can majorly kick my tail in a swordfight."

Buster absent-mindedly fidgeted with the cross that hung from his neck. "She's come a long way since the day her parents died."

Jamie nodded again. "She vowed to never let the Waruiyatsu catch her off guard again." He cleared his throat, not wanting the discussion to go down that road. "Speaking of training, did you bring your nunchuks?"

Buster patted the back of his hips. "I keep them in my belt under my shirt." Jamie had started teaching Buster to use the *nunchaku* shortly after his sensei had taught Jamie the use of the weapon. Buster had picked up on it quickly.

"We're gonna do some sparring while we're here?" asked Dave.

"I'd hoped to," responded Jamie.

"All right!" bellowed the big teen. "Maybe we *will* have some fun this weekend!"

Chapter Four
Friday, 5:37 PM

The home of Tanemura Funakoshi and his great niece, Yoshika Funakoshi, was a beautiful, brick house that was surrounded by perfectly-trimmed shrubs and beautiful, deciduous trees during the summer. In the fall, the lawn was a blaze of autumn color.

Jamie stepped upon the front porch, followed by Dave and Buster, and pressed the dimly lit button next to the door. He could hear the doorbell sound within the house and footsteps running toward the door. As it opened, the three grinned.

The young kunoichi was a vision. Her long, black hair fell to her waist and her bangs were cut straight across. Her slanted, brown eyes alluded to her heritage. Full, red lips framed a row of smiling teeth that couldn't possibly get any whiter. Her arms, visible in the tank top she wore, were slightly muscled. They weren't "body-builder" large, but attractively slim, and the three boys had seen her use them to put enough force behind a punch to knock out teeth.

She smiled at them. "Are we ready to go?"

"The other guys are in the van," responded Buster.

She stepped out and closed the door, checking the knob to make sure it was locked. "Zack and Pete?"

"And B.J.," grumbled Dave.

Yoshi's smile left. "B.J. is here?"

Buster's smile faded, as well. "My mom made me bring him."

Yoshi rolled her eyes and shook her head. “That is unfortunate.”

Buster’s eyes narrowed defensively. “You know, Zack bothers more of us than B.J..”

Jamie knew that Yoshi always spoke her mind. And she continued, “But B.J. always ruins *your* fun.” She patted him affectionately upon the cheek. “I just want you to have a good time, that is all.”

Buster seemed to soften at this. “I appreciate that. But I’ll be fine.”

“Very well,” she muttered, obviously unconvinced. She embraced each of the three, lingering on Jamie.

Zack’s voice sounded out from the minivan. “Hey, toots! Stop with all the huggin’! We wanna go skating!”

Yoshi pulled reluctantly away from her clan brother. Eyeing Zack with contempt, she muttered, “I am going to get near him on that rink floor and trip him.”

* * *

The song was a slow one. Shawna thought it was an eighties song by Tiffany. The teen sat on the bleacher, watching the dancing couples in boredom. Of all of the girls who had come to this dance, she was the only one not wearing something revealing. Well, there was Steve Adams’ girlfriend, Leslie Leigh, but the tomboyish girl who was competing with her own boyfriend for valedictorian of their class had worn pants. Even Shawna’s cousin, Amy, had worn a dress that totally went against school policy, with its low-cut neckline. She supposed that the teachers all realized that, if they sent all of the non-complying girls home, there would not be much of a dance left.

Shawna's eyes settled upon Laura and John, moving slowly to the music. "What does she see in him?" she wondered aloud.

"He's cute," replied Amy simply.

Shawna turned to her cousin, her eyes narrowed. "You're disgusting."

Amy crossed her arms indignantly. "At least she has a date, which is more than I can say for either of us!"

Shawna looked back at her friend and John, who had finished their dance and were walking over to the two girls. "I'd rather be alone than date him." She sighed. "And why don't you have a date? Any number of guys would have loved to have taken you."

Amy shrugged. "Maybe I'm too picky."

As John and Laura came to stand next to Shawna and Amy, John wrapped his arm around Laura's waist and nibbled on her ear, apparently enjoying the glare of disgust that Shawna gave him. "What's'a'matter, Shawna? Couldn't get a date?"

Shawna crossed her arms and looked him in the eye. "I wasn't asked by anyone, if that's what you were wondering."

At this, Freddy came walking forward, handing a glass of punch to John. "Maybe you should have come with Jamie Raleigh," commented the follower. "'Nerds of a feather.'"

"Jamie was having company tonight," replied Shawna.

Laura spoke up. "Leave her alone, Freddy."

"Let'im have his fun, Laura," ordered John.

Shawna rolled her eyes when Laura lowered her head in defeat. The honor student looked over at her cousin, who was now staring intently upward. “What’s wrong?”

Amy squinted, as if trying to bring something into focus. “There are people up there.”

“What?” Shawna looked toward the ceiling. Sure enough, there were several figures crawling around in the rafters.

John had looked up by now, as well. “Maybe they’re fixin’ somethin’.”

“In the middle of a dance . . . in a room that’s lit only by the colored lights from that machine and from the disco ball?” quizzed Shawna, as if talking to a child.

At that moment, each of the figures dropped to the floor on very thin ropes. There was the sound of metal on wood as each figure pulled a short, straight-bladed sword from a sheath at his waist . . ..

* * *

Yoshi skidded to a halt next to the table where Jamie, Dave and Buster sat to enjoy their hot pretzels. Dave looked up at her in the flashing lights of the rink and smiled his normal, friendly smile. “Sorry, dudette. I got ya a soda, but I forgot that ya don’t like root beer.” He had to raise his voice to be heard over the MC Hammer music.

Yoshi seated herself next to Buster, across the table from Jamie. She grabbed Jamie’s pretzel and pulled a piece of it off. “I do not ingest tree bark. But it is no trouble. I will get a Sprite.” She stuffed the warm, soft pretzel piece into her mouth.

Dave asked, "So, where wuz yer uncle tonight, dudette?"

Yoshi finished chewing her bite and swallowed it, then responded, "He is at a Bible study. He goes every Friday night. He has it with several of the men from our church in Aurthur."

Dave shook his head in awe. "That is so weird."

Buster shot him a glance. "What's so weird about it?"

Dave looked at Buster apologetically. "Not that bein' a church-dude is bad, but ya just don't expect t'see the leader of a ninja clan as a religious dude."

Jamie now joined the conversation. "Actually, the ninja were religious, per se. They just weren't Christian. The *kuji kiri*, or *kuji no in*, were originally brought over from the Mikkyo sect of Buddhism."

Dave eyed Jamie as if his cousin had just grown an extra head.

The young male ninja explained, "The ninja hand symbols that all the old eighties ninja movies used to say 'focused the ultimate power of purpose.'"

Dave rubbed his chin absently. "Do you use these symbols?"

Jamie shook his head. "Nah. Master Tanemura taught them to me because they are part of our clan's culture. But, since he converted to Christianity, he doesn't believe that they hold any real power."

Jamie looked around the rink to see what his younger friends were doing. He noticed Zack and Pete doing some stunt skating while holding on to each other's wrists. They would crouch and spin two and, sometimes, three full circles together so fast, the young ninja could tell that, if either released his hold, both would go flying backward. At least Zack was not hitting on every girl in the place.

B.J. had latched onto a video game and was in danger of using all of his spending money.

Yoshi brought Jamie's attention back to the table. "So you gave up going to your school dance to be here with us tonight." She was smiling playfully.

Jamie shook his head, smiling sarcastically. "Trust me, it wasn't much of a sacrifice."

Dave looked at Jamie, his eyebrows raised. "Why not?"

Jamie sighed and took a sip of his root beer. "I have a few good friends, but the rest of the school pretty much follows a guy named John Bowers as if he were a shepherd and they were sheep . . . or something."

"So?"

"He's the school's star basketball player and everyone wants to *be* him. He decides what's cool for all the students . . .," Jamie's face distorted in disgust, " . . . and what's not."

Dave caught on to what was being said. "And, t'him, you and yer friends ain't cool."

Jamie nodded.

"Ya know, if ya smack'im around a little bit, he might just lose that popularity." Dave slammed his right fist into his open left palm for emphasis.

Yoshi responded, "He has kept his training a secret from those at his school."

Buster looked at his friend and mentor. "Why?"

Jamie answered his student with a question, "Do you remember when it first came out in Jameston that I was learning ninjutsu? Remember all the people who used to try to pick fights with me, and the few who wouldn't leave me alone until I did fight them?" At a nod from Buster, he continued, "I don't want to have to fight like that anymore. If I never have to get into a real fight again, it'll be too soon for *me*."

* * *

At the eastern bridge, the black, Chevy van came to a stop. The sliding passenger-side door opened and four black-clothed figures climbed from the vehicle, carrying four civilians. The strangely dressed men carried their bound and gagged prisoners, which included one man and three women, away from the Chevy and toward the northern end of the bridge. As they arrived, the four figures were unceremoniously dumped to the ground.

Two of the antagonists backed away as one leaned over and pulled a short dagger from his belt. One of the four bound figures, a high school teacher by the name of Tim Brown, glared at the armed man. His attacker's eyes lit up with humor at his attempt at bravery.

"Do not fear," said the man, as he cut the ropes that bound Tim's hands. "We are not going to kill you." His accent sounded Asian. "Of those we took at your dance, we are releasing you adults for a purpose."

When Mr. Brown's hands were free, he reached up and pulled the gag from his mouth. "What about the students?" he demanded.

The man sliced the ropes that bound his feet as he replied, "They will not be harmed as long as you follow our instructions and the ones for whom we are looking come to the school."

Tim rubbed his wrists. "And what are your instructions?"

The man with the knife looked at one of the other three and said something in his native language. That one reached into the vest he wore over his suit and produced a scroll, then handed it to the first man. The man turned back to Tim and gave him the rolled parchment.

"Our instructions are written here in English, but there is a note that is only in Japanese. This is for the eyes of our enemies alone. Have this shown on the television, and they will know what to do. But be quick. The deadline is midnight."

The man rose and followed the other two back to the van. After they had climbed in, it made a U-turn and sped back toward the town.

Tim looked at his watch. It was 8:30 PM. He swore in frustration. After untying the three women-the English teacher, Mariah Black; his wife; and Mrs. Tanner, an elementary teacher who had volunteered to help with the dance-he asked, "Is anyone hurt?"

The three women each indicated that they were unharmed.

"Good," said Mr. Brown. "Because we're going to have to walk at least a mile before we get to the nearest house to use the phone. And any news crews that come'll have to drive all the way from the Bluff. They haven't given us much leeway to get this done . . . ."

Chapter Five
Friday, 10:30 PM

Jamie slid from his place at the table and pushed himself into a slow roll toward the refreshment counter of the skating rink so that he could get a refill on his root beer. He looked at his watch. It was 10:30. They would need to be heading back to Sera soon.

He glanced up at the television that hung over the refreshment stand in time to see Tim Brown being interviewed. He couldn't hear what was happening, but Mr. Brown had a few cuts and bruises on his face and his eyes were filled with worry. Jamie felt a sense of dread settle in his stomach at the sight of his teacher. *What happened at the dance?*

Next, a note, in Japanese writing, was shown. "Yoshi!" he yelled.

His fellow ninja was standing next to him in an instant. "What is the matter?"

Jamie gestured toward the television and her gaze followed. As she read the note, her eyes widened. "We must gather the others and get home at once!"

Jamie looked at her in frantic puzzlement. "What did it say?"

"I will explain on the way. Let us just hope that we can reach Uncle Tanemura!"

* * *

Pain. Steve's head swam in the steady throbbing. He felt as if he were in the deepest part of the ocean, with the pressure of the water bearing down upon him. He was smothered. He couldn't see. But, somewhere in the distance, he could hear voices. At first, he couldn't figure out what they were saying. After a short moment, the single word became clear. He was hearing two familiar voices calling his name. He listened intently, determined to follow them to their source . . . determined to leave his sea of pain.

The oppressive darkness ended as he slowly opened his eyes to see . . . his girlfriend, Leslie, and his younger brother, Max. The two helped him to sit up. He rubbed a lump on the back of his head, looking around the room to find that he was in the women's locker room with the rest of the students that had come to the dance. "What hit me?" he groaned, memories of the strange men in black costumes flowing back to him.

"A ninja," replied his younger brother matter-of-factly.

"A *what*?" demanded Steve.

Max stood. "A ninja." He looked down at his brother, folding his arms across his chest. "You know, those Japanese assassins Jamie's always reading about."

Leslie sat cross-legged and put Steve's head in her lap. "I don't think he'd ever want to see one up close," she muttered.

Steve narrowed his eyes as he realized that his younger brother, a junior high student, was with them. "Wait a minute . . . what are you doing here?"

Max smiled his mischievous smile and said, "I snuck into the dance"

"Why?"

Max seated himself on a bench next to another student. "Why else? To bother *you*."

"And if you hadn't, you'd be safe at home now," argued Steve. "See, that's why Mom's always telling you that you shouldn't do things just to annoy me!"

Max rolled his eyes. "Yeah, I'm sure she expected something like an army of ninjas to attack your high school dance."

* * *

Jamie sat in the middle of the center seat of the minivan, leaning forward between Buster and Yoshi, in the front, bucket seats. "So, you want to let us in on the big secret?" he demanded of his clan-sister.

Yoshi sighed, reaching up and rubbing her eyes wearily. "I caught something about evacuating Sera and for the enemies of the people who wrote the note to be at the school by midnight, or they will start killing the hostages."

Buster appeared confused. "Who are their enemies?"

Yoshi looked at him. "The note bore the seal of the Warui jonin."

Jamie rested his forehead on his right hand, his elbow propped on his right knee. "We're the enemies."

By now, Dave had leaned forward next to his cousin in the middle seat, unusually quiet. After a moment more of silence, Jamie ordered, "Buster, turn on your radio to 96.9."

"Why?" was his student's response.

"That's the closest radio station to Sera. It's in Doniphan. Maybe they have something on about what's going on."

Buster reached over and flipped on the radio. Static rattled as he tuned in the station Jamie had asked him to find. The newscaster, Del King, was speaking, " . . . *has been evacuated from the town, per the instructions on the note. The county sheriff's office has requested a language expert from the governor to decipher the Asian wording on the note. The governor hasn't yet stated whether or not he will be requesting military troops in the area at this time. Again, an army of 'strangely dressed, Asian men,' as quoted from Tim Brown, has taken over Sera high school and, now that Sera has been evacuated, the town, as well. We'll keep you posted of any further developments as they occur.*"

Jamie interlaced his fingers and rested his chin on his knuckles, deep in thought. Finally, he spoke. "Even without telling anyone my secret, I've still put my classmates in danger."

Yoshi looked back at him compassionately. "You cannot place blame upon yourself, Jamie. The Waruiyatsu have long been known to do things of this nature. If not to get to *us*, then to gain wealth, or power, or notoriety."

* * *

The remaining thirty minutes of the trip from the Bluff to Aurthur went quietly. The older members of Adventure explained the details of what was going on to the younger, then everyone sat silently in the van, lost in his or her thoughts. The tension in the van had been palpable and Jamie was almost relieved when they reached Yoshi's street.

As the van pulled into the driveway of the Funakoshi's house, she swore. "Uncle Tanemura is not home yet," she said in frustration. As soon as Buster placed the vehicle in "PARK," she leaped from the passenger's side and burst toward the front door, followed closely by Jamie and Dave. She reached into her pocket and fished out her house key, shoving it into the doorknob and turning it. The door swung open and the three walked inside.

Yoshi rushed to the living room phone and dialed the house where the bible study was held. "Hello, Mrs. Wagner? This is Tanemura's niece. Is he there, by chance?" There was a pause as the person on the other end spoke. Jamie watched Yoshi's face contort in panic, but the feeling didn't creep into her voice. "Okay. Thank you." She placed the receiver back on the jack. Looking at Jamie, she declared, "All of the men in the group but Uncle Tanemura and Mr. Wagner have food poisoning. It was apparently bad meat. He has taken them to the emergency room." She sighed. "I suppose that it is good that Uncle does not like pork."

Jamie walked over to the cabinet upon which the phone sat and opened one of the side-by-side doors. Reaching in, he pulled out a phone book and flipped through the pages until he found the hospital's phone number. He grabbed the receiver from Yoshi and dialed it.

A voice answered, "*Southern Missouri Regional Medical center. How may I direct your call?*"

"Emergency room, please," replied the young ninja.

After a few clicks, a familiar voice answered, "*Emergency room. This is Cheryl. How can I help you?*" Cheryl had admitted Jamie's father for pneumonia so many times that the woman could quote their address.

"Cheryl? Can you tell me if you admitted a bunch of men with food poisoning tonight?"

"*Hi, Jamie!*" exclaimed the middle-aged woman. "*How is your dad?*"

"He's fine," replied the young man impatiently. "But it's really important that I find a Japanese man that was with the men who were brought in tonight."

"*You know, now that you mention it, I do remember them.*" She typed a little bit. "*Yes, six men were admitted tonight for food poisoning.*"

"And the Japanese man who brought them in?"

"*He stayed here for about an hour to see if they were okay,*" she continued, "*but he just left.*"

"He just left?"

"*Not five minutes ago.*"

"Thanks, Cheryl."

"*Tell your dad I said 'Hi.'*"

"Will do." He hung up. Looking up at the other two, who had been joined by the rest of the group from the van, he said, "He just left."

Buster looked at his watch. "Let's see, it took us half an hour to get here from the Bluff and twenty minutes to get here from Jamie's house. It's a quarter after eleven now. If we wait for Tanemura, that won't give us enough time to get to Sera before they kill the first hostage."

Jamie glared at him. "What do you mean by *we* and *us*?"

Dave looked at his cousin. "C'*mon*, dude. Yer pretty good at that ninja stuff, but you and Yoshi, and even Tanemura, can't fight a whole clan'a ninjas."

"*Ninja*," declared the male ninja, emphasizing the end of the word. "The plural form of *ninja* is *ninja*. And this isn't your fight."

Buster spoke up. "It became our fight when those jerks killed Yoshi's parents." He looked at her apologetically for bringing it up, then continued speaking to Jamie, "They were good people and some of the only members of your clan who didn't treat us *western* kids like barbarians."

"Yeah," continued Pete, "and we proved we're capable of fighting the *Wara-whoosits* that day, too."

The group now looked at B.J.. "What are we supposed to do with the shrimp?" asked Pete.

B.J. shot his brother a glare and squealed, "I'm goin' with ya."

"Oh, no you're not!" corrected Buster. "Mom and Dad are gonna be mad enough when they find out *I* went."

"We could drop'im off at Jamie's house," suggested Pete.

"I'm goin' with you!"

The group ignored B.J. as Jamie responded, "We can't. My parents are home by now and they'll wonder where we're going this late at night." He sighed. "I've never been good at lying. You guys know that."

Yoshi jumped in. "We will simply leave him here." She had been writing a note for her great-uncle. "He can explain everything to Uncle Tanemura when he arrives home."

"I'm going with you!"

"Good idea, Sis," said Jamie.

B.J., by now furious at being ignored, kicked his brother in the shin as hard as he could. "I'M GOING WITH YOU!"

"OOOOWWWWWWW!!!" exploded Buster, hopping around on one foot.

Jamie glared at the child. "*You* are staying *here*, whether you like it, or *not*." He placed his right hand on B.J.'s shoulder. "We're doing this for your own good. And we need for you to tell Master Tanemura what's happening."

B.J. slumped his shoulders in defeat. "Okay."

"But he's only nine," commented Zack. "Is it really safe to leave him here by himself?"

Jamie and Dave met each other's glances. He knew that his larger cousin was having the same idea. "You stay with him," the young ninja instructed Zack.

Zack's eye's widened. "That wasn't what I had in mind . . .."

"But dude," interrupted Dave, "do you really wanna go fight ninja?"

Zack thought about that for a moment. "Good point."

Chapter Six
Friday, 11:23 PM

On the opposite end of the gym from the locker rooms was a small office. Coach Bevlin, absent during the dance and attack, covered the walls of this room with awards that he had won while he was in high school and college. To most students, the framed certificates that wallpapered the room, leaving very little empty wall space, would be impressive. But to the sinister man in the black suit who sat in the coach's chair, examining a *shuriken*, it was just a bunch of useless paper.

The door to the office opened and a familiar voice said, "There is still no sign of the Funakoshi, Master Obata."

The jonin of the Waruiyatsu arose from the seat and stood at his full height of 5'10", impressive for a member of their clan. "You have posted watches on the eastern bridge?"

"We have, Master."

"They will come." He continued to examine the throwing star that he held. "They are such sentimental fools. I suspect that the *gai-jin* has friends in this school. He will not allow them to be harmed."

"Our spies had seen the American ninja conversing with a few of the students who are held in the locker room, Master."

Obata turned to look at his subordinate and raised an eyebrow. "Indeed?" His lips parted into an almost friendly smile. "Well, we should make the friends of the chunin of the Funakoshi clan feel more comfortable, would you not agree?"

"What are your orders, Master?"

Obata turned away from the other ninja, examining the dartboard on the far side of the room, and stated, "I am leaving for our base by the river. I leave the matter in your capable hands."

The other ninja, his voice tinged with excitement, said, "Yes, Master!"

"Separate these 'friends' from the rest in the locker room. If you have to begin killing prisoners, start with them."

He turned his head to watch the other ninja bow in compliance. As the chunin turned to leave, his leader's voice stopped him. "Tanemura is to be taken alive, Kuzuki." He turned back to the dartboard, hurling the shuriken. "His niece is to be killed, but do this mercifully. She cannot help that karma has chosen her to be the one to bring about our fall.

"As for the gai-jin . . .," he turned back to the dartboard, where the throwing star now shined in the bulls-eye, "you can make him suffer before you kill him."

* * *

The door to the locker room creaked open and two of the ninja stepped in. One of them pointed in turn at George, Max, Steve, Jeremy and Shawna and said, "You five will come with us."

"Why?" asked Steve as he climbed to his feet.

The ninja who had spoken appeared agitated and responded, "If you must insist upon asking questions, then we will be forced to sever your tongue."

Steve defensively covered his mouth with both hands.

Leslie leaped to her feet and grabbed Steve's right arm. "No!" she yelped.

The ninja who had been silent this whole time stepped forward and began to pull a dagger from his belt, but was stopped by the other. "We are not to harm them!" he snapped. The speaker looked at Leslie almost compassionately and said, "I have a wife and child. I know the pain that you feel now." He gently removed her hand from Steve's arm and continued, "I assure you that he will not be harmed if our demands are met."

Steve cupped Leslie's face in his right hand and, using his thumb to wipe a tear from her eye, whispered, "It'll be okay. I'll be back." He kissed her, then turned to follow the others out of the room, trying his best to ignore her sobs.

* * *

Jamie and Yoshi wore their ninja uniforms. The suits consisted of black pants, a vest, and detachable arm coverings that fit over the back of the hand and were held in place by a black loop that fit over the middle and ring fingers. Their boots, called *tabi*, were also black, with a split between the big toe and the rest.

As the two walked around the weapons room in their teacher's house, gathering up what they would need, Jamie began to worry about his parents. How would they react to what he and his friends were about to do? He knew that they were proud of his sense of responsibility, yet he also realized that they hated the concept of him being in danger. They had been relieved, but angry, when he and the others had battled the Warui ninja at Yoshi's parents' home. How would they react now?

The young ninja shook his head and sighed. "I'm glad that we don't have to go to my house to get my ninja suit."

Yoshi smiled. "I suppose that you are pleased that your young friend, Max, found it and asked you about it?"

Fortunately, Tanemura had enough weapons to arm a legion of ninja. They had each grabbed a crossbow with a quiver of bolts, several throwing stars, a couple of handfuls of caltrops (*tetsu-bishi*), and a few smoke balls.

Finally, Jamie grabbed a ninja-to and sheath from the wall. He examined the sword that he had chosen. Like most ninja-tos, its blade was two feet in length and straight, not curved like the *katana* of the samurai. The hilt was wrapped in either shark or eel skin (either way, it was probably imitation, considering the fact that these swords were made in the twentieth century) with a black cloth braided over it. This last feature was for added grip rather than decoration. He wished he had his personal sword, crafted by Deck Pendragon especially for him. But it was the one weapon that he had kept at his house.

Yoshi had developed a style where she used two of the swords. This was self-taught, as neither Jamie, nor even Tanemura, could use two of the weapons at the same time. Proud of his niece's ingenuity, the jonin of the Funakoshi clan had commissioned Deck to craft two of the ninja-tos with Yoshi in mind. Each was balanced perfectly for her and was an inch shorter than a normal ninja-to.

Jamie looked at Yoshi and asked, “Are we ready?”

She sighed, a look of steel resolve on her face. “We are ready.”

“Then let’s get the others.”

* * *

Jamie was relieved that most of the others hadn’t taken their suitcases out of Buster’s van before they had left the young ninja’s house for the Bluff. Dave had thrown his entire bag in Buster’s van, rather than digging out his skates and leaving the bag behind.

Each was armed and ready. B.J., who sulked on Tanemura’s couch, and Zack, who sat next to him, watched the others gather around Jamie and Yoshi. The palpable emotions could be felt by everyone in the room, taking different forms for each person. Worry, fear, and even excitement were here.

Dave wore a pair of camouflage army pants with black army boots. His muscles rippled under the plain, white T-shirt he wore under a black, leather vest. Various fighting, hunting and survival knives were sheathed on his elastic belt, on his pant-legs, and on his boots. The outfit was completed with a navy blue headband.

Buster wore a pair of white, drawstring pants that were a part of a karate uniform. He had chosen white jogging shoes and a black T-shirt. Two pair of nunchaku, were sheathed in black, leather straps around his legs. His small, silver cross gleamed from the chain around his neck.

Pete had changed into a black jumpsuit. He wore a matching sweatband and his white tennis shoes.

Buster cleared his throat. "I know that you guys don't always like to hear about religious stuff, and all that." He sighed, and then continued, "But I just wanted to offer a little group prayer, considering the situation."

Yoshi gently took his hand. "You know that I will gladly accept prayer."

Jamie took her other hand and nodded to Buster.

One by one, all the members of the group grasped hands until they were standing in a circle. Buster, Yoshi on one side and his brother on the other, prayed, "Holy God of Heaven, we give You praise for the relationship that we share. Each of us feels a bond to one another that is stronger than normal friendship. We are a family . . . a family that You, in Your infinite wisdom, have brought together.

"Lord, lead us in the endeavor in which we now strive, to free those who have been kidnapped. Help us to be a beacon in the darkness . . . and keep Your protective Hand on us." Buster took a deep, shuddering breath, then continued, "In Your Son's Holy Name, Amen."

Each of the rest of the group followed with an *Amen* of his or her own.

Buster wiped his hand across his eyes. "Now I feel a little better about walking into the lions' den."

* * *

The five sat in metal chairs. A raised area, the place where they were sequestered was often used as a stage when they turned the gym into an auditorium. Tonight, the only thing that was there was the stereo system that had played the music.

George looked at Steve and asked, "Why do you think they singled us out?"

Steve thoughtfully pinched his bottom lip. "I'm not sure." He looked around at the other four. "I can't see what we all have in common that would interest these people." He gestured at Shawna. "She, Max and I are honor students, but that would leave out Jeremy and yourself." He gave a friendly smile. "No offense intended."

"None taken," said George.

Steve continued. "Max and I are brothers, but there are no family ties between the three of you, and I fail to understand why they would care about that, anyway."

He looked at George again. "You knocked a few of them around with the handle of the mop that Mr. Brown had used to clean up Freddy's vomit. That might have caught their attention. But it doesn't explain us."

George looked at Jeremy. "Maybe you yelling, 'I'm Robin Hood!' got their attention."

Jeremy smiled self-importantly until Shawna offered, "I'm surprised that they didn't mark him a lunatic and kill him on the spot."

Steve was just about to ask George where he'd learned to fight with the mop, when the silent ninja came forward. "It is ten minutes until midnight," he hissed. "You had better hope that your friend gets here before then, or one of you will die."

The five looked at him with a mixture of fear and confusion. "Wh . . . what friend?" demanded Shawna.

The ninja just shook his head and turned away.

Steve was really perplexed. "What friend of ours could interest these ninja?"

"How about Deck?" offered Jeremy. "He's a pretty good fighter."

"And more of a nut than *you,*" remarked Shawna. "Besides, he was supposed to be at the dance tonight. If they wanted him, they could've just waited a little longer and he would've shown up."

"How about Jamie?" asked George.

"What would a ninja clan want with Jamie?" asked Max. "Besides, I wouldn't exactly call Shawna his *friend.*"

The other three males each raised an eyebrow at him as Shawna blushed.

Chapter Seven
Friday, 11:50 PM

Buster pulled the minivan into the parking lot of the high school building. Jamie climbed out of the vehicle, his feet crunching on the loose gravel of the lot. He pulled his glasses case from a pocket in his vest and opened it, making sure he had remembered to put his glasses inside when he had changed into his contacts at Tanemura's.

Dave walked up to stand next to his cousin as the young ninja slid the case back into his vest. The big teen sniffed the air playfully and declared, "I smell a majorly AWESOME BATTLE comin', dudes!"

Yoshi walked up to the two boys and sighed. "I wish that we could have reached Uncle Tanemura," she said.

Jamie put his mask on. "Surely he's heard the news by now. He's probably on his way here as we speak."

"Jamie's right," agreed Dave. "I'm sure B.J. and Zack've told him everything by now."

* * *

Tanemura Funakoshi hung his car keys on the rack next to the back door. He walked to the refrigerator and opened the door. Reaching in, he grabbed a can of *V8* and opened it.

Taking a swig, he thought about his trip home from the Bluff. An accident had blocked traffic on Highway 67. An eighteen wheeler had wrecked, falling onto its side and stretching out the width of the road. The old ninja didn't know what had caused the accident, as his car had blown a fuse earlier during the day and the radio would not turn on.

He walked past Yoshi's room, noting that the light within was off and the door was ajar. Apparently, she had decided to sleep at Jamie's that evening. "Your father would never have approved of you spending the night with a bunch of boys," he whispered. But he was too exhausted to be angry. He would just need to speak to her about what was proper the next day.

He stepped into his bedroom and closed the door. Had he bothered to look in the living room, he would have found Yoshi's half-finished note on the television. He would have also found the two boys, sleeping peacefully on the couch and loveseat.

* * *

The group of teens moved silently through the shadows surrounding the school building. Jamie strained to hear anything out of the ordinary, but all he could hear were the feet of his friends, crunching on the autumn leaves that had settled upon the sidewalk.

"Why aren't we tryin' the front door?" whispered Dave.

"They'll have it well-guarded," responded Jamie.

"As if they would leave any path clear," commented Yoshi.

"True," returned Jamie, "but they went through an awful lot to get us here just to keep us from getting in."

They came to the set of metal doors on the west side of the building. On either side of them were two large, glass windows. Pete cupped his hands over his eyes and leaned his face up to the glass.

"Pete!" whispered Yoshi harshly. "You would make an excellent target for anyone inside!"

"Relax," he returned. "I don't see anybody in there."

Dave grabbed the metal door handle and pulled. The door opened. "This is too easy, dudes."

Jamie walked past him and entered the dark corridor of the building that ran along one side of the gym, moving a few feet to peer into the windows of one exit to the large room. He saw about twenty black-clothed figures walking around the gym, talking with each other. Two more stood guarding the door to the girls' locker room. Looking down, he could barely see a thick chain and padlock locking these doors. He groaned under his breath and looked back up and into the room.

His heart jumped into his throat. Max, Jeremy, Steve, George and Shawna were seated on the stage, separated from the rest of the students. He caught his breath and turned away from the door. The Warui must have been spying on him for quite some time. They had easily picked out his friends, and even his *crush*. Looking back into the window, he noted two ninja, one wearing the necklace of a chunin, approaching the five. The other started to reach for Steve, but the chunin stopped him and grabbed Max instead. Jamie looked quickly at his watch, which read *11:55 PM*.

Looking up at the clock that was on the opposite wall of the gym, he read the time as midnight. He almost swore. “It’s five minutes fast!” he exclaimed, despite himself.

Yoshi was at his side in an instant. “What?”

Jamie looked at her frantically. “They’re going to kill Max Adams!”

Dave looked at the doors. “Don’t think I can break these down.”

“There’s another way in,” suggested Jamie and he turned and lunged down the hall.

The group followed him about a hundred feet up a ramp before the wall to their right that enclosed the gym turned away from them, forming the northern wall of that large room. Jamie ran along this wall until he came to an old, brown, wooden door. Taking hold of the handle, he turned it to find that it, too, was locked. He looked up at Dave. “No time to pick it.”

The big teen moved back several spaces to give himself a little running room . . ..

* * *

“Well, young one,” commented the ninja with the strange necklace shaped like a *Y*. “Apparently, your life is not valued by your friend.” The other ninja held Max’s hands behind his back as the speaker pulled a knife that was a miniature version of the ninja’s sword from a sheath on his belt. “Please do not take this personally.”

“Of course not,” replied the teen, his voice cracking with terror and undermining his attempt to hide his fear with sarcasm.

George, Steve and Jeremy leapt to their feet, but several of the ninja grabbed them and pinned them back into their seats.

"Please don't do this," pleaded Shawna, her eyes welling with tears. "He's just a kid."

"Yeah," said Max, his voice cracking. "I just crashed the dance!"

A BOOM that thundered through the gym brought everyone's attention to the northern entrance. Standing in front of the doorway was a group of adolescents. Two familiar outfits stood out from the others as the two ninja who were with the group stepped forward.

"*Funakoshi,*" whispered the ninja with the dagger, his right hand tightening around the handle of the weapon in anticipation. His eyes narrowed as he called out, "Where is the other one?"

One of the two masked warriors, a female with two swords strapped to her back, answered, "My uncle could not be reached." Her hands grasped the handles of the two ninja-tos. "I hope that we will provide enough entertainment for you."

"We shall see." The attack party leader's voice was now tinged with humor as he dropped his knife and whipped out his own sword, calling out, "Waruiyatsu! Kill them!"

Chapter Eight
Friday, 11:59 PM

Ten of the ninja charged the bleachers over which the northern door to the gym opened. Jamie reached into the vest of his ninja suit and produced two marble-sized metal balls and then hurled them into the midst of the charging shadow warriors. As they hit the floor, they exploded into clouds of smoke. Looking over the ninja throng and rising smoke, he noticed Max slam his foot down upon the foot of the ninja that was holding him. As his captor released him in shock, the young martial artist's same foot shot backward, connecting with the ninja's gut and sending him flying off the stage.

Jamie's ninja-to leapt from its sheath as he plunged from the bleachers and into the fray.

Dave jumped to the floor, narrowly dodging a blade as it swung in a downward arc. He grabbed his opponent's wrists before he could pull back for another strike. Looking into the eyes of the shadow-warrior, he good-naturedly exclaimed, "How'ya doin', dude?" He brought his knee up forcefully into the ninja's stomach and the sword clattered to the floor. Wrapping his massive right arm around the ninja's neck, with the top of the head facing behind him, the big teen fell backwards, slamming his captive unconscious.

Four ninja surrounded Buster, who had one pair of nunchaku ready. He eyed each of them warily, waiting for them to make a move.

They all charged at once.

The kensai began swinging his nunchaku around his body, switching hands and flailing outward to the front, back and sides, the weapon moving so fast it could barely be seen. By the time he had finished the maneuver, all the warriors were laying at his feet.

Yoshi blocked the blade of a charging ninja with one of her own, swiping at his unguarded stomach with her other sword as he rushed by. Her right foot lashed out catching another in the face and knocking him from his feet. Spinning her right ninja-to to grip it underhanded, she shoved it backward, taking out another warrior who was preparing to attack her from behind.

Pete ran from two ninja, the adrenaline pumping through him making him feel as if his feet were barely touching the floor. He slid under the buffet table, which stood at the base of the stage, and leapt to his feet on the other side. The two ninja stopped on the side of the table opposite him, eyeing him cautiously.

One of them jumped over the table, but didn't quite make it over before one of Pete's well-placed kicks slammed into his face, knocking him backward. He slid off the table, taking the punch bowl with him and dumping its contents onto him.

Another boy, the one Jamie had called Max, leaped from the stage and landed on the table.

"What are you doing?!" demanded one of the older boys from the stage. "You're going to get hurt!"

The second ninja who had been chasing Pete swiped at Max's ankles with his ninja-to. The boy jumped over the attack, kicking the ninja in the face as he did so.

"This is our chance!" Max yelled back at the boy. He looked down at Pete and said, "You have to excuse my brother. He doesn't like anybody to hurt me but himself." Then Max looked toward the end of the gym and his eyes widened in shock.

Pete turned to see three more ninja at the opposite end of the gym, each pointing a loaded bow at them. He swore at the shadow warriors as Max jumped behind the table and the two turned it on its side just in time to catch the arrows in the top. The food fell onto the floor and the sound of glass shattering echoed through the gym.

The ninja with the bows charged the overturned tables. Jeremy grabbed the folding chair that he had been sitting on and slammed it shut.

"What are you doing?" demanded George.

"Those look like nice bows," responded the young Robin Hood fan as he swung the chair with all his might, catching one of the ninja in the head as he ran by, knocking him from his feet.

The other two ninja, noticing their comrade had just fallen, tried to stop their momentum. But their feet slid in the spilled punch, they flailed their arms and fell hard on their backs.

Jeremy held the chair in front of himself and yelled, "BANZAI!!!" as he leaped off of the stage and landed on the ninja that he had struck.

Dave ran by, clothes-lining another ninja as he did so. Looking at the stage, he called out, "Where're the rest of the students?"

A girl with glasses and bleach-blonde hair pointed to the western side of the gym and responded, "They're in the locker room!"

"Thanks!"

Another ninja, wielding a spear, rushed the big teen. Dave moved to the side, catching the weapon and tugging it out of his attacker's hand. He dropped it, doubled over, wrapped both arms around the ninja's waist, then stood straight and fell backward, slamming the warrior, head-first, into the floor.

Another ninja went down with one of Jamie's well-placed cuts. He was starting to feel nauseated. Killing wasn't exactly something that he was used to. He'd felt the same way when he'd killed that one ninja at Yoshi's parents' home . . ..

"RALEIGH!!!" Jamie turned to see one of the ninja, his eyes narrowed in hatred beneath his mask as the blade of his sword pointed at the teen. Judging from the necklace that he wore around his neck, a pendant that was shaped like a *Y* with sharpened points, he knew this opponent to be a chunin like himself. Jamie's ninja-to moved out into a defensive stance as his eyes narrowed.

The two rushed each other, their swords meeting violently as they passed. Jamie instinctively swung his blade backwards, blocking an attack in the process. Whirling around, he pressed an attack on the other chunin with a downward swipe, which was narrowly dodged . . ..

From his position on the stage, and with all of the commotion that was going on in the gym, had Steve heard correctly? Had the leader of these ninja just yelled out the name "Raleigh?" He looked at his two companions who were still on the stage with him, the same look of puzzlement etched on their faces.

Steve looked back at the combatants. Their fight had just taken on a whole new meaning . . ..

Dave knocked on the locker-room door. "Is everyone okay in there?"

He heard a girl's voice say, "Yeah."

Dave called back, "We're here ta help! Back away from the door! I'm gonna break it down!"

The same voice from inside asked, "Is there still a guard on the door?"

Dave started to back up. "No!" he yelled in answer.

He started to lunge forward but barely caught himself as the door swung outward and a pretty, blonde-haired girl peeked out, her deep-blue eyes settling on the big teen.

"Is it safe?" she asked.

A male's voice from inside demanded, "Laura, get back in here!"

The girl called back into the room. "It's okay! I think we're safe!"

Dave shook his head to clear it and looked around, noting that Jamie was battling with the last of the ninja.

Their blades continued their lethal dance, the sound of metal striking metal resounding through the gymnasium. It almost seemed to Jamie as if he and the other chunin were merely watching the weapons in their battle . . . bystanders in a mindless war.

The leader of Adventure ducked an attack and shoved the tip of his blade into the Warui ninja's foot. His enemy grunted in pain as Jamie struck his sword arm with the flat of his blade, sending the other chunin's sword flying. The teen spin-kicked his opponent across the face, bringing him to his knees. Jamie grabbed the ninja by the vest and brought the point of his ninja-to his throat.

"Do it, gai-jin," demanded the other as he reached up and weakly removed his own mask, forcing Jamie to look him in the face. "Kill your enemy. Kill him, as our kind have always done."

Jamie's eyes narrowed. "I'm NOT your kind!"

The other ninja smiled bitterly, revealing bloody teeth. "The Funakoshi have blood on their hands as well. How many lives have you already taken this night?"

Jamie trembled. Anger? Guilt? "I never wanted this." He slammed the fist that was holding his sword across the other ninja's face and felt the warrior go limp.

"DUDE!" called Dave. "Not *bad*!"

Jamie looked at his cousin to see that he had freed the rest of the students. Buster stepped up to him and asked, "You okay?"

Jamie nodded, but his eyes betrayed his conscience.

His student patted him on the shoulder. "They didn't really give us a lot of choice."

Yoshi walked up to Jamie's other side and asked, "And what of the survivors?"

Jamie looked around, figuring that they had about six prisoners. "We killed that many?"

The kunoichi sighed. "It could not be helped."

Jamie wiped the blood from his blade on a piece of cloth produced from his vest pocket. "Strip them and tie them up." He looked back and forth between his two friends. "We want to make sure they don't have any hidden weapons.

"As for the dead ones," he shuddered, "after Buster's said a prayer over them, we'll clear a section of the cafeteria's freezer to put them." At his friends' stunned looks, he added, "it's a really big walk-in freezer and there should be enough room to keep them separated from the food. And we don't want them to be rotting here in the gym."

Yoshi gestured toward the freed prisoners and declared, "I believe that they are awaiting an explanation."

Jamie glanced at the group that now stood behind Dave, each regarding the young ninja and his friends curiously. Suddenly, Steve Adams stepped forward. "It *can't* be!" His eyes widened. "*Jamie*?"

Jamie threw a glance at Dave, whose face darkened as he nodded. The young ninja let out another sigh as he slowly removed his mask.

The dead quiet of the room was palpable. Jamie looked over his Sera friends, each barely breathing with this sudden revelation. His eyes took in the other students. Each of them stared at him in shock. No one moved. No one blinked.

Then John Bowers swore. "What is this, Raleigh?"

The sea of students parted as the jock made his way toward the ninja. Jamie did not move at all as John came to stand directly in front of him. Bowers's alcohol-laden breath filled Jamie's nostrils.

Then John grasped Jamie by the collar. "What've you gotten us into?"

"John," groaned Shawna, "I knew you lacked a brain, but this is ridiculous!"

Jamie looked at Dave, who began to step forward to play his role as Jamie's bodyguard, but the chunin stopped him with a glare.

John ignored all of this as he continued his bravado. "Ordinarily, I'd consider it beneath me to dirty my hands on you but, this time, I'd be doing the other students a disservice if I didn't."

Jamie's hand shot up, grasping the wrist that was holding him and viciously twisting until John released him. The jock let out a yelp as Jamie used his right foot to sweep both of John's from underneath him. The bully landed with a painful THUD, staring at the young ninja in fearful amazement.

"I'm through playing games with you, Bowers," declared Jamie, fighting to hold his anger in check. "Remember earlier today, when you asked me where I'd learned to do what I did to Freddy?"

John opened his mouth to speak, but he couldn't seem to force any words out.

Jamie continued. "I learned from a man named Tanemura Funakoshi . . .," he pointed to the kunoichi, " . . . Yoshi's great-uncle and the leader of the Funakoshi ninja clan.

"Until now, I was content to let you think that you were 'everything,' and I was 'nothing,' just to keep from having to fight, which I hate to do. But, with the Warui ninja present, I had no choice but to reveal myself."

"What do they want with you?" asked Shawna.

"Our clan has been at war with the Waruiyatsu for nearly five hundred years," explained Yoshi. "The Funakoshi came to America to leave the fighting behind, but they followed us." She removed her mask and she continued, "Our clan is led by my family, from whom the clan gains its name. Should all of our members be killed, then the next family to take leadership will be the Shokato, the largest family. They are as violent as the Warui and, thus, most in our clan do not approve of them. If they were to take leadership, it would most likely cause a civil war."

Buster looked at Jamie. "So what do we do now?"

Quickly counting the students, the young ninja answered with a question. "Do you think you can drive a school bus?"

* * *

Dave bounced heavily in his seat in the front of the long, yellow vehicle as Buster hit another bump in the road. “Hey, dude,” bellowed the big teen, “watch the road! Where’d you learn how t’drive?”

“Hey,” snapped Buster defensively, “gimme a break. I’ve never driven a bus before!”

Dave rubbed his bottom and muttered, “I can tell!”

Jamie, sitting across the aisle next to Yoshi, watched this exchange with some humor. It felt good to smile.

Max’s voice caught his attention. “So what’s gonna happen to the ninja that you guys tied up in the coach’s office?” The junior-high student had leaned over the back of their seat with his head perched between those of the two ninja.

Jamie turned around and replied, “Hopefully, once we get out of this town, they’ll send in some army guys . . . or something.”

“So I guess the ninja suit *wasn’t* just a collectible, huh?” pressed Max.

Jamie just smiled and shook his head in response.

“How often do you practice?”

“Yoshi and I get together three times a week,” explained Jamie. “I’ve also built an obstacle course in the woods behind my house.”

Then he and Yoshi slammed into the padded wall behind the driver’s seat as Buster hit the brakes.

“HEY!!!” exclaimed Max as he flew over the seat to land between Jamie and Yoshi, his head between the seat and the padded wall and his legs sticking up in the air.

"Guys . . . ," began Buster warily.

Jamie stood and moved to stand next to him, bending slightly so that he could see out of the front window. He could hear Yoshi swear in Japanese, even as he gasped in shock.

The bridge was gone.

* * *

Buster sat on the bleacher, praying silently. He needed guidance. This was not what any of them had expected. Or was it? No. None of them had even expected to survive the fight, let alone win it.

But the Warui ninja had seen the possibility. After leaving the eastern bridge, the bus had headed back through town toward the Current River bridge. Jamie had not been optimistic, and with good reason. This bridge, too, was gone.

Buster finished his prayer, then looked around the gym. The school was the only place they could think of to go. The Warui prisoners, still tied and stripped to their underwear in the coach's office, had refused to speak when questioned as to how many of their comrades were still free in the town. Yoshi had been the only one that they would even deem to honor with speech. But this was only to remind her that the Warui still had the upper hand.

Then Jamie had come into the room. Buster could still remember the pure hatred that the men had shown for his friend and teacher. But, then again, was it truly hatred? Or could it have been *fear*? That would have made sense. Jamie had shown a fighting prowess far beyond his age when they had first encountered him the day they killed Yoshi's parents. He had killed one of them that afternoon. Easily. He had also nearly taken out their mission leader for trying to kill Yoshi.

Yes, they feared Jamie. This was why they had set the explosives in the bridges. They had expected the possibility of Jamie, Yoshi and Tanemura defeating all twenty of them, even without the wildcards that were the rest of Adventure.

"Hi," came a voice behind him. He turned to see Yoshi. Of course, he realized, only Yoshi could have moved up behind him without being heard on the old, creaky bleachers.

He smiled at her. "Hey, what's up?"

She seated herself next to him. "You simply looked lonely, sitting here all by yourself."

His smile widened. "I'm never alone."

She nodded knowingly. "God is with you."

He patted her on the shoulder. "He's always with you, too." Clasping his hands over his lap, he explained, "I had been praying, actually."

Mirroring his pose, she asked, "Did you get any kind of response?"

Buster sighed, obviously frustrated. "Sometimes His answers are like getting a spiritual anvil dropped on my head." He helplessly ran his fingers through his hair. "Sometimes, He speaks really softly."

"And you cannot hear Him over all of the noise in the gym."

The young preacher chuckled. "Well, Christ did tell us to pray in a closet."

Yoshi raised an eyebrow. "In the dark?"

"Actually," he explained, "I think He was just trying to tell us that we're not supposed to make a public spectacle of it." His smile widened even more. "Of course, He knew that there would be times like this, too."

"And it doesn't bother you to pray in front of people?" Her tone was curious, not accusing.

He shook his head. "Nope. I won't deny my Father before man."

* * *

Jamie dropped the phone back onto Mrs. Brown's desk, not even bothering to put it back on the cradle. This was the last phone in the building. And, like the others, the line was dead.

"Why do you suppose they're not working?" asked Max, who had gone with Jamie and Pete for a way to contact the outside world. "The lines coming into the school look unharmed."

"They probably did something to the phone company," reasoned Pete. "There probably isn't a working phone in the whole town."

"So what are we going to do now?" asked Max.

Jamie sighed as he ran his fingers through his light brown hair. "I guess we're going to camp in the school. We'll post watches in shifts and discuss our options with everybody in the morning."

As the teens filed out of the room, Jamie could hear Max telling Pete, "Jamie could've really saved himself a lot of trouble if he'd told everybody this big secret of his when he first moved here."

Jamie sighed. He knew that it was not that easy.

Chapter Nine
Flashback
September 11, 1986
Thursday, 1:48 PM

The office was frigid. Jamie's nose was cold. He half expected his breath to come out as steam.

Next to him, Dave cracked his knuckles as he looked toward the door to the principal's office. The big teen sighed, then dropped his hands onto his lap.

The steady tapping of the secretary's typewriter formed a chorus in Jamie's head in time with the pounding of his migraine. He sighed, reaching both hands up to rub his temples.

"Dude," whispered Dave. "You got nothin' t'be ashamed of. Dennis had it comin'."

Jamie glanced down at his gray *Batman* t-shirt. Dark spots were already drying on the fabric. Drops of crimson marred the yellow of the bat insignia. He had no illusions that he would ever be able to wear this shirt again.

The door that led to the hallway opened and Jamie's parents walked in, followed by Dave's mother and Tanemura. Dave's mom, Lynn, settled her gaze on her son. "Who'd you beat up this time?" she demanded.

Dave's eyes widened. "Me? I'm innocent, Mom."

Lynn crossed her arms and regarded her son coldly. "And I'm supposed to believe that?"

Jamie's mother, Pam, looked at Jamie. "What happened? Is that blood on your shirt?"

"It's not my blood," responded Jamie. "Dennis Long wouldn't leave me alone and he tried to hit me in the face with my math book."

"So Jamie creamed'im," finished Dave.

The three parents looked at Jamie in shock, while Tanemura sighed.

The principal's door opened and he stepped out, followed by a red-faced woman with a dark perm. "Mr. and Mrs. Raleigh?" Mr. Banton said as he extended his hand. Jamie's father, Chuck, shook it.

Mr. Banton opened a manila folder that he was carrying. "This is a highly shocking case, I must admit." He looked down at Jamie, his eyes narrowing. "Until today, Jamie hadn't so much as gotten a tardy for class."

"I don't care what his background's like!" yelled the woman who had followed him out of the office. "He broke my son's nose! What are you going to do about him?"

At that moment, the door Jamie and Dave's parents had just come through with Tanemura opened and Mr. Filker, the middle school Social Studies teacher, stepped in.

"I'm a little busy right now, Fred," said Mr. Banton to the newcomer.

"If it's about the fight, that's why I'm here," regarded the teacher calmly.

The principal's eyes widened. "You want to shed some light on what happened?"

Mr. Filker nodded. "I saw the whole thing. Dennis has been picking at Jamie all year. Jamie has held himself in check the whole time until Dennis physically attacked him today."

Mrs. Long's eyes bulged. "If my son attacked this one, then why isn't he hurt?"

Tanemura now spoke. "I have been training Jamie to defend himself."

Mr. Banton regarded Jamie calmly. "Is this what happened?"

Jamie nodded. "I don't like to fight. As long as he was just insulting me, I didn't let it bother me. He'd been doing it ever since everybody found out about my training."

"And my son isn't going to get into trouble with us for defending himself when a kid tries to hit him," stated Chuck.

Jamie looked at Mrs. Long. "I didn't mean to hit him that hard. I just wanted to make him stop attacking me."

Mr. Filker laid his hand on Jamie's shoulder. "Dennis swung at him several times before Jamie finally stopped warning him."

The woman looked around at all the adults present, then finally sighed. "I can see he's going to get away with it."

"No more'n yer son gets away with on a daily basis," grunted Dave.

Gathering her dignity, Mrs. Long pushed past the assembled adults and walked out of the room.

Jamie risked a glance at Tanemura, who mouthed the words, *We'll talk later.*

Chapter Ten
November 17, 1991
Saturday, 2:37 AM

"Mind if we take a seat?" asked a pretty girl with bleached-blonde hair who stood next to an attractive brunette.

"Of course not," smiled Yoshi. "You two are on Sera's Quiz Bowl team, are you not?"

The brunette nodded.

Yoshi's eyes narrowed in thought. Pointing at the girl with the blonde hair, she said, "You are Shawna Westin and this is your cousin, Amy."

Shawna smiled. "Good memory."

"Not half as good as yours," returned the kunoichi. "You stomped us in our last match."

Shawna blushed. "Well, we have a good team."

The two Sera teens took a seat, then sat in awkward silence for a moment, before Shawna finally asked, "So, where's Jamie?"

"He went with his cousin, Pete, and Steve Adam's brother to see if any of the phones were working," explained Buster.

"Are we still hoping to get out of here tonight?" asked Amy.

"You mean, *this morning*?" asked another Sera girl who climbed the bleachers with Max's brother. Her brown hair was cut just below the neckline and she appeared to be the only girl who had worn pants to this dance.

Yoshi narrowed her eyes in thought again. "Leslie Ringstaff."

Leslie smiled and nodded.

The female ninja noticed that Shawna was looking at the cross she was wearing. “Is something troubling you?”

“You’re wearing a *cross*.”

Yoshi cradled the holy symbol in her right hand. “And you want to know why a ninja would wear a Christian symbol.”

Shawna shrugged. “I’m not meaning to be rude, or anything.”

“My family was the first of our clan to come to this country,” explained Yoshi. “My uncle came many years before my parents and I followed him.” She smiled at the memory. “He converted to Christianity soon after his arrival, when he was in his mid-twenties.” She shrugged. “My parents and I went with him to his church in St. Louis the weekend after our arrival. My father and mother accepted Christ that very evening and I was simply raised from that point with our Savior being a fact.”

“Wow,” commented Amy, “a Christian-ninja family!”

“Is Jamie a Christian?” asked Leslie.

“He believes in God,” responded Yoshi. “As do his parents.” Her brow furrowed. “He does not go to church, though. His mother *used* to take him, but that was before his father got sick.”

“With emphysema,” concluded Shawna.

“Yes.” Yoshi regarded her curiously. “You know much about him.”

Steve closed his almanac. “They’re friends,” he explained.

Amy chuckled. “Friends? I think they want a lot more than friendship!”

Shawna smacked her cousin in the shoulder with the back of her hand, then turned away, her face bright red.

“It’s true,” commented a blonde boy who climbed the bleachers and took a seat next to Steve.

“I’d smack *you*, George, if I could reach you,” stated Shawna indignantly.

Steve Adams looked at Yoshi and changed the subject. "Ever since I've seen you at Quiz Bowl, I've wanted to ask you something."

Yoshi looked at him expectantly.

"Isn't *Yoshi* a boy's Japanese name?"

Buster chuckled as Yoshi smiled politely and explained, "My given name is *Yoshika*, but I have always been what you American's call a tomboy. It is my preference to be called *Yoshi*."

At that moment, Jamie and the other two teens that had gone with him walked in the door Dave had knocked down. They approached the flock of teens that were surrounding Buster.

“Any luck?” asked the kensai.

Jamie shook his head. “They didn’t want to take any chances.”

“What are we going to do now?” asked Shawna.

“I guess we’ll wait out the night here,” replied Jamie. “Some of my friends and I’ll take turns at watch through the night. We'll decide on another plan tomorrow morning."

"DUDES!!!" Dave called out from the stage to no one in particular. "I got it working!" He was still fidgeting with the stereo.

"Your cousin's cute," commented Amy. "Personality *and* a bod. A winning combination."

Jamie chuckled. "And he's an accomplished fencer."

Jamie's smile turned to a cringe as the sound of feedback echoed through the large room. He looked up at the stage to see Dave operating the dials of the sound system. As Jamie and his friends watched in fascination, Dave stood and walked to the front of the stage, turning his back to the students.

"When did he change into his blue Hawaiian shirt?" asked Pete.

"While you guys were looking for a working phone," replied Buster.

Suddenly, the words, "I'm too sexy . . " filled the gymnasium. Most of the students went ballistic as Dave began to dance and lip-sync to *Right Said Fred*'s hit. He flowed with the music, doing dances that coincided with the words, which seemed to make the girls in the room squeal with delight.

Jamie looked around at the students, amused by how much they were enjoying the spectacle of his outgoing relative performing for a group of strangers. Even Laura Blanton, who was sitting at the far end of the bleachers, had her eyes glued to his cousin. The young ninja cracked a smile, until he watched John Bowers walk up to the cheerleader and grab her forcefully by the shoulder and say something to her. She flushed and turned away, her head lowered.

Jamie climbed to his feet and started to make his way toward the couple. For the past year and a half, everyone had sat by and let the basketball player beat her into submission. But the young ninja no longer had anything to hide. He would sit idle no more.

Shawna caught his arm and shook her head. He sat down beside her and put his ear up to her face so he could hear her over the music. “She'll resent it if you interfere,” she explained. “Trust me. I know.”

Jamie looked back at the two and now noticed that she had her head lying on his shoulder, his arm around her. With a sigh, Jamie nodded his understanding. It would, eventually, be Laura who would have to stand up to his abuse. Then, he noticed that she was grimacing in pain, but saying nothing, as John dug the fingers of his left hand into her left arm. The young ninja hoped that she would have the sense to do something before it was too late.

The song finished to a standing ovation. Apparently, Jamie and Shawna had been the only ones to see the exchange between the basketball player and cheerleader.

Dave stood on the stage with the index finger, pinky and thumb of his right hand extended into the "I love you" symbol. The cheering was deafening.

Jamie smiled. He wished he had his cousin's confidence.

* * *

Jamie lay awake on the cold, hard science room floor. Dave snored peacefully next to him. The big teen had brought a sleeping bag along and had unzipped it so that he could flatten it out for both to use. But Jamie couldn't sleep. He wasn't cold, though the students hadn't been able to find much in the way of blankets. Each classroom had a temperature control and Jamie and Dave had set theirs for seventy-five.

Jamie examined the towel that he'd procured from the Home Ec room upstairs. He had rolled it up into a pillow. It was soft and comfortable. This wasn't it, either. "How do you get *any* sleep in a situation like this?" he whispered to himself.

Then he thought back to his childhood, when his mother would kneel beside him at night and he'd say his prayer. He hadn't prayed in so long. Truth is, until Buster's group prayer tonight (or, rather, last night), he hadn't prayed in over two years. He closed his eyes, trying to remember that old bedtime prayer. "*Now I lay me down to sleep. I pray my Lord my soul to keep . . .,*" he prayed softly. It was a child's prayer, but he didn't know how else to do it, so he wasn't embarrassed. After all, who could hear him but God?

* * *

Yoshi walked along the wall that ran inside the northernmost side of the school building. Her watch had been pretty uneventful. She hadn't heard a thing in the forty-five minutes she'd been making her rounds. Of course, where ninja were concerned, the quiet could be quite misleading.

There were a few *chinking* sounds ahead, then a rather loud THUD. With her left hand, Yoshi secured the ponytail tie that had her hair in a bun, pulling a ninja-to from its sheath on her back with her right. Silently, she padded forward.

* * *

George had suffered from insomnia when he was young, though he thought he had gotten over it. He supposed that tonight was a strange exception. He was hot, due to the fact that the heat in his room had been raised to compensate for the lack of blankets. This heat prompted thirst, which is why he now stood outside the science room, in front of the soda machines.

He picked up his *Dr. Pepper* and opened the can. Moving it to his lips to take a drink, he dropped it and yelped as a shorter figure lunged around the corner that connected this hall with the northern one, ramming him up against the soda machine with the blade of a sword to his throat. He relaxed a bit when he noticed that it was Jamie's friend, Yoshi.

"What are you doing out here?" she demanded with a sigh as she slid her ninja-to back into its sheath.

"I'm sorry," he offered. "I was really thirsty."

"Wasn't there a water fountain closer to your room?"

George stooped over and picked up his soda, which had miraculously landed bottom-down, spilling nothing. "I get enough water at home. My parents only cook *health* foods."

Yoshi chuckled. "This is a bad thing?"

George groaned. "If I ever eat another soy burger, it'll be too soon."

The kunoichi raised an eyebrow. "Do you eat the school's food?"

"Yeah but their food isn't made of soy protein," he responded. "It's made of radioactive waste."

Yoshi laughed.

Chapter Eleven
Saturday, 5:07 AM

The jonin of the Funakoshi ninja clan sat straight up in his bed. What had awakened him? Then he heard the ringing again. He sighed. "You are getting too jumpy in your old age, Tanemura," he chided himself as he reached for the telephone's cordless receiver.

He hadn't quite gotten it to his ear when he heard a familiar woman's voice. "*Tanemura?*"

"Yes, Mrs. Raleigh?" He usually enjoyed talking to Jamie's mother, but not at five o'clock in the morning. Just because Jamie's father had always risen at the crack of dawn didn't mean that everybody did. "It is rather *early* . . .."

Pam interrupted him. "*Is Jamie there?*"

He was completely awakened by that question. The old ninja ran his fingers through graying hair as he responded, "I thought that they were at your house."

Jamie's mother took a shuddering breath. *"Haven't you seen the news?"*

"I took some sick friends to the hospital last night and the radio in my car shorted out," he replied as he climbed from the bed and, putting on his robe, padded into the living room. "Why?"

He reached for the television and turned it on to see a cartoon. He started flipping through channels.

"An army of ninjas have taken over Jamie's school!" exclaimed Mrs. Raleigh.

Tanemura nearly dropped the phone. "WHAT?!"

"It's all over the radio!"

"Now calm down, Mrs. Raleigh . . .," Tanemura began, but was interrupted by a loud SNORT behind him. He whirled to see a child sleeping upon his loveseat and an adolescent sleeping on his couch. "B.J.!" He was really beginning to think that his age was finally catching up with him. "Zack!"

Buster's brother lurched into a sitting position. "Wh . . .What?" he asked groggily.

"Is it morning already?" groaned Zack as he took one of the sofa pillows and covered his head with it.

Tanemura rested his right hand firmly upon B.J.'s shoulder. "What are you doing here?"

B.J.'s eyes settled on Tanemura and flashed recognition. "Mr. Funakoshi! There are ninja at the school! And they wanted you and Jamie and Yoshi to come or they were gonna kill the students, but JamieandYoshicouldn'tgetaholdofyousotheywe . . .."

"Slow down!" called Zack's muffled voice from under the pillow. "You're gonna rupture somethin'!"

B.J. took a deep breath. "There are ninja . . ."

"I caught that part," interrupted the ninja master.

"Jamie and Yoshi couldn't reach you so they went with the others to try an' rescue the students."

"Mr. Funakoshi?"

Tanemura put his ear back to the phone. "Yes, Mrs. Raleigh, I am still here." He walked hurriedly toward Yoshi's bedroom.

"Who were you talking to?"

"I was speaking with B.J.."

"B.J.'s there?"

"And Zack. They were sleeping in my living . . .," he trailed off as he pushed open the bedroom door to find an empty bed. But what scared him the most was that the sword rack at the foot of that bed was also empty. "Oh, Heavens!"

"*What?*" Jamie's mother demanded.

Tanemura rubbed his forehead with his left hand. "Mrs. Raleigh, I think that I should come to your house immediately . . .."

* * *

The large man checked his massive sword. He had lovingly crafted this weapon himself and, in keeping with his fascination with medieval history, had given it a name . . . *Blade.* So it wasn't original, but that was about the only thing that wasn't original about this person.

He looked down at the clothes that he now wore. He had removed the more fashionable button-up shirt, replacing it with a black T-shirt when he had gone back to his house to get his weapons after seeing the ninja blow up the bridge. He had never tried to swim in a kilt before, but he prided himself in his Scottish heritage and would never dream of going into a fight without wearing it.

He pulled a large pistol from his belt. He'd named it *Dragonfire.* No sense in getting the weapon wet during his swim and he wasn't going to let a little water deter him from helping his friends. If Jamie, Yoshi and Tanemura had gotten to the school, then the students were probably free. But he had to prove this to somebody. More than their substitute art teacher, he considered himself Jamie and Yoshi's friend.

He had noticed what he hoped was an army encampment upriver a mile or so from where the bridge had been. The man hoped to get some help there. But first, he had to get across.

Taking a deep breath and holding the gun above his head, he waded out into the frigid water of the Current River on this November morning . . ..

* * *

B.J., Zack and Tanemura stepped onto the large, flat concrete slab that served as Jamie's parents' front porch. "Jamie's brother kicked that in the door," explained the preteen, gesturing at the footprint imbedded in the wood.

"Yes, I know," answered Tanemura absently as he raised his fist to knock.

He never got a chance. Jamie's mother opened the door. Lines of worry crisscrossed her forehead.

"Have you heard anything?" asked the jonin.

"The news said that an army regiment's been dispatched into the town, but they aren't doing anything yet," answered Mrs. Raleigh.

"We shouldn't know that much!" commented an enraged man from the couch behind her.

"It is good to see you again, Donnie," offered Tanemura to Dave's father. Jamie's mother moved to the side and the jonin and children stepped into the house.

Jamie's father sat in his recliner, Chico on his lap. Tanemura smiled politely and scratched the old dog behind the ear.

"How are you doing, Tanemura?" Donnie climbed to his feet and extended his hand.

Tanemura shook it. "I have been better, I would say." He shook Mr. Raleigh's hand and asked Mr. Isaac, "Why did you say that we shouldn't know about the troops?"

Dave's father's brow furrowed. "They've broadcast it on every channel! If we know the army's in the town, then those ninjas know!"

"Do you think Jamie and the others went up there?" demanded Mrs. Raleigh.

The old ninja sighed. "By all appearances, they did."

Jamie's mother covered her face with both hands and began to sob.

"Pam, I'm sure they're fine," comforted Chuck.

"I can't help it," cried his wife. "My baby's up there!"

"That *baby* of yours is a ninja," reminded Donnie. "And all of those kids are more than capable of taking care of themselves."

* * *

Sometime during the night, Jamie had fallen asleep. As he opened his eyes, the morning sun washed into the room through the many-windowed wall on the east side.

Jamie sat up on the sleeping bag, finding his cousin still snoring peacefully. *Let him sleep*, he thought. *He's going to need all his strength today*. Jamie stood and looked at the clock on the wall over the chalkboard. It was ten minutes after nine.

Climbing to his feet, Jamie spent about ten minutes doing standing stretches, then another ten doing sitting stretches. He spent fifteen minutes in meditation over the events of the previous night. Then he tapped Dave with his foot and asked, "Do you still have that extra toothbrush?"

Dave sat up and ran his hands through his shoulder-length, curly brown hair and answered, his voice still filled with sleep, "Yeah, it's in my pack."

Jamie snatched his cousin's army green bag from the teacher's desk and began to filter through it. He pulled out a tube of toothpaste and found a new toothbrush, still in the package. He silently opened it, then put some of the paste on it. Walking to the sink, he began to brush his teeth.

"Ya think anybody else is up?" asked Dave as he started doing a set of push-ups.

Jamie responded, but Dave couldn't understand him with the toothpaste in his mouth.

"Huh?" responded the big teen.

Jamie spit into the lab sink, then said, "I saw some people walking over to the cafeteria."

"Ya think Buster's already over there cookin'?" grunted Dave as he completed his tenth push-up.

Jamie gargled with water and then spit. "Probably," he replied. As he rinsed the toothbrush, there was a light tap at the door.

Dave climbed to his feet, moving his shoulders in circular motions to loosen the tightness of sleeping on a hard floor. He walked to the door of the room and opened it to find Yoshi. "Good morning, handsome," she said with a smile.

Dave bowed elegantly. "And a top'o'the mornin' ta *you*, dudette."

Yoshi walked into the room. "I was just about to head to the cafeteria to have some of the preacher's gourmet cooking," she offered, "and I was just wondering if you two handsome gentlemen would like to escort me."

Jamie smiled and put the toothbrush back into Dave's pack.

Dave answered her. "We were just headin' that way, ourselves, and we'd be delighted to join ya."

The three walked out of the room, one boy on each arm of the attractive young woman. They exited the northeast door of the building, which was right next to the science room. Autumn was working in overtime, painting the trees vivid colors of red, yellow and orange.

"Did I hear you talking to somebody in the hall during the night?" asked Jamie.

"Yes," replied Yoshi. "I spoke with your friend, George."

"Why was he up?" asked Dave.

"He was thirsty and wanted to purchase a soda," was the reply.

"How long did you guys talk?" inquired her clan brother. "I think you were still talking when I fell asleep."

"We spoke until the end of my shift."

Jamie nodded. "Interesting guy, huh?"

Yoshi smiled. "He is actually quite charming."

The three teens arrived at the double-doors to the cafeteria. The brick building stood next to a twin structure that served as the band room.

Jamie grabbed the handle to the right door and pulled it open. He could hear the students talking, as they always did when they came for lunch. One almost had to yell to be heard. The addition of someone playing Vanilla Ice's "Ice Ice Baby" on his boom box didn't lessen the noise.

As the three entered the building, the students, without exception, stopped talking and looked at them. The two boys and girl looked around in confusion. The only sound that could now be heard was the rap song.

Dave, at the back of the three, turned to see if there was anything behind them.

Then, the students began clapping.

Jamie's face flushed red, as did those of his two companions, as they made their way quickly to the counter where Buster was serving food. To get there, they had to pass between two long tables. To his left, he noticed John Bowers, Freddy Jenks and Laura Blanton. The latter was smiling meekly, though not clapping. The former two were glaring at the three, though John's focus seemed to be on Dave.

"Dude," commented Dave to Jamie as they each picked up a tray. "Has that guy considered a laxative?"

"He's just jealous of the attention you got for your performance last night," explained his cousin.

"You mean this *morning*?" corrected Yoshi.

"Uh, yeah." Jamie let Yoshi get her food before him. "Anyway, he was really upset that his girlfriend was enjoying the show."

"Really?" asked Dave, his interest piqued. "*She* liked it?"

Jamie looked at his cousin in amusement. Did he like this girl? He hadn't given his affections to another since Traci Bundy in Jameston . . .. "Well, he *is* her boyfriend."

Dave looked back at the basketball player and narrowed his eyes. "She deserves better'n that creep."

The young ninja shook his head. "You don't know the half of it."

Dave moved his attention back to Jamie. "Huh?"

As Buster used an ice cream scoop to put a helping of scrambled eggs on Jamie's tray, he looked back up at his cousin and replied, "Let's just say that even she's not immune to his temper."

"You guys sleep okay?" asked Buster. "You had the only room in the building that didn't have carpet."

Jamie gestured to Dave. "He brought a sleeping bag, so we just unzipped it and flattened it out."

Buster slid a tray of food toward Jamie's cousin. "Dave?"

"Huh?" Dave, who had been looking back at John and Laura, jumped.

"You want the gravy on your eggs?"

"Uh . . . yeah, I guess."

Jamie patted his cousin on the shoulder. "I'll meet you at the table."

"Don't forget to give thanks," commented Buster.

Jamie smiled, giving Buster a "thumbs up," and walked over to join the rest of Adventure.

Buster spooned an extra-large helping of gravy over Dave's eggs. "Back for seconds, gentlemen?"

Dave looked at Buster quizzically, until he noticed that he was talking to someone who was behind him. He turned to find John and Freddy.

"No," replied the basketball player. "We just wanted to have a chat with the hero here."

Dave cocked an eyebrow and leaned back against the counter, folding his massive arms across his chest. "S'up?"

"Quite the show-off, ain't ya?" asked the jock.

Dave shrugged. "I've been accused o' worse."

Freddy put his left hand, large in its own right, tightly on Dave's right shoulder. "Stay away from John's girl."

Dave looked back and forth between the two, barely keeping himself from bursting out in laughter. Were these guys joking? His gaze settled on John.

Dave's right hand shot up, grabbing Freddy by the wrist and, his eyes never leaving the jock, squeezed painfully until the bully let go. Then Dave shoved him back a step. "Here's a thought for ya, dudes." His gaze bore into John. "Jamie don't like to fight, which is the only thing that's kept you two from pickin' yourselves up off the floor on a daily basis."

He picked up his tray, then continued, "I'm not like my cousin. I love nothin' better'n bustin' a few heads." He smiled darkly. "And I have absolutely nothing against layin' you out right here in front of all these people and showin' them what a spineless loser you really are . . .," he bowed mockingly, his eyes never leaving John, " . . . your majesty."

He turned to leave, but found his way blocked again by Freddy. "Dude," muttered Dave. "You're breathin' my air." He then sniffed and continued, "And your breath stinks. Haven't you ever heard of a toothbrush?" He shouldered past the bully and walked toward his friends.

Left at the counter in front of a snickering Buster, John looked speechlessly after Dave as Freddy attempted to nonchalantly breathe into his right hand and sniff it to see just how bad his breath really smelled.

Chapter Twelve
Saturday, 10:01 AM

Dave plopped into his seat to Jamie's right. "That dude's got a major butt-kickin' comin'!"

"I think it's safe to say that you spooked him," muttered George from his place on the far side of Yoshi.

"Wow," commented Shawna, who had arrived with Amy and now took a seat across the table from Jamie, "I've never seen anybody stand up to John like that."

"He had it comin', dudette," muttered Dave as he jabbed his fork into his eggs. "I never did anything to him."

"That's never stopped him before," said Amy.

"My fist in his mouth'll stop'im in the future," mumbled the big teen as he shoveled the fork-full of food into his mouth.

"Anyway, he's not mad at you because you did anything wrong, per se," explained Shawna. "He's mad because Laura took such an interest in you."

Dave looked up at her, the corners of his mouth curving into a smile that he could not hide. "Really? She did?"

Amy took a bite of her eggs. "Hey! Where'd he get real eggs?" The school used a powdered egg product.

"He didn't," replied Pete, between chews.

"Then how did he get'em to taste like real eggs?" was Shawna's cousin's next question.

Jamie swallowed his second bite. "He just has a knack for cooking."

Amy looked to the head of the room to see Buster taking off his apron in preparation to join his friends. "Cute and he can cook. A winning combination."

Jamie and Shawna each looked at her. "I thought you said that 'personality and a bod' were a winning combination," murmured Shawna.

Amy smiled at her cousin. "Men have so *many* winning combinations, don't they?"

Steve and Max Adams and their friend, Jeremy, moved from another table to join Jamie and the others. "Did you consider the *Boat House*?" asked Steve.

"What about it?" Yoshi asked.

"We could use some of the boats from there to get across the river," explained Max.

Buster seated himself across from Steve. "It doesn't seem like a bad idea."

Jamie swallowed his bite of eggs. "While we're in the boats, we'd be sitting ducks. Besides, wouldn't that be stealing?"

"Not really," was Max's response. "Fred Corbett, the owner's son, is a friend of mine."

"As for the danger factor," added Max's brother, "you could just leave some of your friends on the shore on this side of the river to keep us covered. After that, the ones that made it to the other side can keep the people who come across last covered."

"Sounds like a plan," commented Dave.

"But the danger is something that we should all choose for ourselves," countered Yoshi. "Let us put it to a vote."

Without another word, Dave pushed his tray aside and climbed on top of the table. As Jamie and the others watched in awe, he called out, "Dudes and dudettes!" Every voice in the room quieted. "This dude," he gestured to Max, "has come up with an idea. He thinks we should get some boats from this *Boat House* on the river and use'em t'get across."

"That doesn't sound like a bad idea," commented Laura Blanton from her place next to John, who glared at her. Under his gaze, she lowered her eyes to the floor.

"Why does it sound like there's gonna be a big 'but'?" asked a sophomore.

Jamie stood. "Like any option we have, it'll involve some risk." He sighed. "Even staying here will be dangerous."

"Then we put it to a vote?" asked Shawna.

"We do," was Jamie's reply.

The young ninja asked for a show of hands. The vote was nearly unanimous, with John, Freddy and some of their friends the only holdouts, in favor of the boats.

As the last two students exited the cafeteria and headed for the bus, they failed to notice the lone figure, dressed from head to foot in black, drop from the rafters of the ceiling . . ..

* * *

The Chevy Blazer raced up Highway 21. Tanemura Funakoshi, from his place in the passenger's seat, glanced at the speedometer. "I do not believe that I have ever seen you break the speed limit before."

"The laws are there to protect people, Tanemura," commented Donnie Isaac. "But my boy's in that town somewhere and I won't rest 'til they're out."

The jonin turned his gaze back to the road ahead. The plan was for the two of them to head east of Sera, then go north toward Doniphan and leave the SUV near the road and hike back west. It was their only hope to get into the town after the bridges had been destroyed.

Thinking they might have to camp, they'd brought Don's camping gear. They were also armed. Don's pump action shotgun and his police pistol were on safety in the back seat. Tanemura was wearing a camouflage ninja suit (minus the mask) and carried his favorite ninja-to and typical ninja weaponry. "I do hope that you will have enough ammunition, should a conflict with the Warui arise," commented the leader of the Funakoshi clan.

"I've got plenty," was the reply. "Don't you worry about that."

They rode eastward in silence for a few moments. Finally, his eyes still on the road, Tanemura again spoke. "Why are you here, Don?"

"What?" Donnie took his eyes off the road long enough to glance at Tanemura. "I'm trying to help you get to the kids."

"That is not what I mean," responded Tanemura.

"Then what do you mean?"

Tanemura's eyes regarded Dave's father coolly.

Donnie cringed under the old ninja's gaze. "I hate it when you do that."

Tanemura raised his eyebrows in feigned innocence. "And what is that?"

"When you give that *you can't hide anything from me* look of yours."

"You are still somewhat early for deer season," commented Tanemura. "You usually only come up to hunt. Otherwise, you visit your sister, leave Dave with Jamie and go home, then come back for him at the end of the weekend."

"How do you know that I didn't hear about the ninja and turn around to come back?"

"Zack said that you rented a motel room in Aurthur," was the response.

"I could have just wanted to spend more time with my sister than I usually get to," said the camouflage-jacketed man defensively.

"The newspaper in your back seat is open to the real estate section and several entries are circled."

Donnie looked at the old jonin in wonder. "Is there anything that you ever don't catch?"

"The flu," smirked the older man. "And I didn't notice the children who were sleeping in my living room until this morning." He smiled warmly. "Jamie would love for Dave to live close to him."

"We were thinking about moving up here," muttered Don. "The police academy has me teaching classes in St. Louis *and* Kennett and that drive's a killer."

"Yes," replied Tanemura. "You used to speak of that when you lived closer to St. Louis and would drive once a month to Kennett." His smile was replaced with a look of concern. "But you moved to Jameston to be closer to Kennett when you were officially transferred there. Why would you move closer to St. Louis now? Are they transferring you back?"

Donnie sighed. "Those three kids who started that street gang are being sent home to Jameston."

Tanemura's eyes widened. "How did you discover this?"

"A friend in the juvenile corrections department in Kennett told me. Said that he figured I might want to spread it to Dave and Jamie and their friends who were fighting with them before they were sent away."

"Have you told the children yet?"

"No." He glanced at Tanemura. "I did tell their parents, though." He set his eyes back to the road. "The Goodmans are considering a move, since Buster's dad doesn't want to run for chief there again. The others are talking about moving, too."

"They will be scattered?"

Donnie chuckled bitterly. "Actually, for safety reasons, everybody's been talking about moving up here."

Tanemura raised a questioning eyebrow.

Don explained, "If those kids are as vindictive as we think they are, we want to get our kids away from them. But what's to stop them from following us? The chief and I have gathered a general consensus that there's safety in numbers."

* * *

Colonel Peters saluted the private who guarded the large prisoner. “Has he said anything, yet?”

The private returned the salute and replied, “He’s been talking since we caught him. He won’t shut up, sir.”

Peters removed his army green hat and rubbed the top of his completely bald head. “Let me in to see him.”

The private obediently opened the flap of the tent and held it so the colonel could enter. Seated in a wooden chair in the center of the tent, illuminated by various lanterns that sat on tables around him, was a large man. His black T-shirt covered a well-muscled upper torso, though one could tell he had a not so muscled stomach, which gave him an almost jolly appearance. This, however, was over-shadowed by the scowl that he wore on his red-bearded face. His muscular arms ended in massive hands that were handcuffed behind his back His large legs were similarly tied at the ankles to the chair. A pair of smiley-face boxer shorts could be seen under the checkered skirt he wore in place of pants.

Peters groaned and stepped forward. “What’s your name, son?”

The man looked at him in irritation. "I've given my name to somethin' like ten soldiers so far this morning."

"Humor me."

The prisoner sighed. "Deck Pendragon."

"Okay, Mr. *Pendragon*," muttered Peters, "what were you doing swimming across the river last night?"

"I was trying to get t'the school. I was s'posed ta be a chaperon for the dance."

"Were you aware that some kind of terrorists have taken over the school?"

"Ninja."

"Now, how the bloody blazes did you know that?" demanded the colonel.

"Head t'toe in black . . . Japanese . . ." recounted Deck. "Shall I continue?"

"You were going to the dance soaked, huh?"

"I was going to fight the ninja. I was hoping to get you guys t'help me."

Peters looked skeptical. "Have a lot of experience fighting ninjas?"

Deck sighed again. "I have three good friends who are ninja."

The colonel's eyes narrowed. "Do they live around here?"

The large man nodded. "Why?"

It occurred to the colonel that this man's friends could be the three enemies mentioned in the note. The fact that a ninja clan had happened to attack a school dance in Southern Missouri was hard enough to swallow. Throw in three more of the blasted assassins and the coincidence was just too much.

Peters examined the prisoner again. "Why are you wearing a dress?"

Deck looked at the officer indignantly. "It's not a *dress*. It's a *kilt*."

Chapter Thirteen
Saturday, 10:57 AM

The bus pulled between the *Boat House* and the office. The office was a small trailer with fake wooden siding to make it look more elegant. Mrs. Corbett had complained about how tacky the former owners were and was always considering the purchase of a new office, but she was so busy with the business and the raising of her son that she never seemed to find the time.

The *Boat House* was actually two warehouse buildings that were each about the size of the gym at the school. One could rent canoes, motorboats, tubes for floating, or lifejackets.

Buster pulled the bus as far back from the road as possible. "Y'know, the ninja aren't very likely to use the road ta look for us," muttered Dave. "It's not like hidin' back here's gonna do us a lotta good."

"True," stated Yoshi. "But Jamie and I are the ones that they want and we will be moving away from the bus to check on the boats."

"I don't feel comfortable with this," commented Buster, his right hand going reflexively to the cross that dangled from the chain around his neck.

Yoshi smiled. "Pray for us."

Jamie looked around, more worried about the fact that they had *not* seen any of the Warui ninja. "Buster, you take the point. Circle around the bus and watch out for anything suspicious. Dave . . .," he looked at his large cousin, " . . . you stay in the bus and guard the students. Max Adams is a pretty good fighter, too. Use him."

Yoshi stepped down the stairs and off of the bus. Jamie followed, but was stopped on the bottom stair by Shawna's voice. "Be careful."

Jamie cocked a half-smile and gave her a "thumbs up." He hoped he looked more confident than he felt.

The two made their way along the gravel that surrounded the two buildings, each scanning the area for signs of any ninja.

* * *

Hidden behind a group of three trees on the side of the warehouse farthest from the office, there *was* a ninja. He watched them with great interest, his gaze moving back and forth from the male to the female.

He smiled cruelly. *I have improved since our last confrontation, gai-jin,* he projected silently. *This time, it is YOU who will be humiliated . . ..*

* * *

Buster walked calmly around the large, yellow vehicle. He swirled a pair of nunchaku in each hand as he prayed silently to himself. So far, he had seen no sign of the ninja. He thanked God for that. Maybe this would be an uneventful excursion after all . . ..

* * *

Yoshi swore in Japanese. "I do not believe this!"

Jamie groaned and ran his fingers through his light brown hair. "I'm not the least bit surprised." He surveyed the wreckage that used to be the inventory of the *Boat House*. "If they blew up the bridge, then don't you think that they'd think to do this, too?"

Yoshi stomped her foot in frustration. "I was hoping that . . .." She stopped, having heard the sound of metal moving ever so quietly against wood . . . the all too familiar sound of blades being unsheathed. And there were many of them. Jamie's alert eyes told her that he had heard, as well.

Jamie's ninja-to leapt into his hand. Yoshi followed suit with one of her own. The two padded quietly outside, their senses on full alert.

"I know I heard that," muttered the boy.

"As did I," responded the kunoichi.

Without warning, a dozen ninja came running from the office. Another dozen leaped from the top of the warehouse. Another two dozen splashed out of the river. Each had his blade drawn.

"Back to back!" commanded Jamie as he and his clan-sister moved into a defensive position.

"Twenty-four to one," commented Yoshi as she pulled her second blade. "Dave would like these odds."

"Well, *I* don't," murmured Jamie as he pulled his *shinobi-to*, a miniature version of the ninja-to, from its sheath at his hip.

With that, the Warui attacked . . ..

* * *

Dave sat sideways in the driver's seat, his head resting back on the side window in boredom.

"What's taking them so long?" wondered Shawna aloud.

"I think I just saw something!" called Jeremy from the back of the bus.

"What?" demanded Max.

"My reflection!"

George groaned. “Can’t you take anything seriously?”

“Why would I want to?”

“Maybe because my cousin’s in danger right now,” replied Pete.

“No more than us,” was Jeremy’s response.

Pete, however, was not looking at him. He was looking past Jeremy at the space between the trailer and the warehouse. “I just saw a ninja.”

* * *

Buster circled around the front of the bus. He’d lost track of the number of times he had done this. He prayed ceaselessly, interceding for Jamie and Yoshi. As he circled around the bus this time, he caught a glimpse of a black-clothed figure moving from the office to the warehouse. Then he saw another. Then another. Finally, he stopped counting at eight as he yelled out, “DAVE!!! START THE BUS!!!”

The engine roared to life as Buster turned about and, after two long strides, jumped aboard the vehicle. He was thrown against the front of the top step as Dave slammed the bus into reverse and shot it backward, then into first, circling around to face the two buildings.

"Watch it!" yelled the kensai, as he climbed into the aisle. "You're going to kill us before we ever get to them!"

"Don't worry, dude," replied Dave calmly, though his steering of the bus was anything but calm. "I know what I'm doin'."

Buster was knocked into the seat behind the driver's seat, landing across Amy and Shawna's laps. Looking up at Amy, whose stomach his face had been buried in, he blushed and said, "I'm really sorry."

She just smiled.

Climbing to his feet, Buster yelled at Dave, "You're gonna hit those boards!" Indeed, the bus bounced over an area of 2X4s that were being used to repair some damage to the back of the warehouse in the off season.

Many of the students nearly bounced out of their seats.

Dave grabbed the microphone to the bus's intercom and his voice could be heard over the bus. "Ladies and gentlemen, this is yer captain speakin'. We're experiencing some turbulence . . .." The bus hit some more boards and the big teen could be heard muttering, "That can't be good on the axles."

"Where'd you learn how to drive?" raged Buster as he finally settled into the empty front seat to the right of the girls.

Dave's smile nearly took in his ears. "From Army dudes in tanks! Best teachers in the world!"

Buster rolled his eyes . . ..

* * *

Jamie worked his blades furiously. The shinobi-to, he used for blocking, saving the longer ninja-to for striking back. The Warui field ninja, known as *genin*, weren't particularly skilled when compared to the two Funakoshi *chunin*, but there was a veritable army of them.

He risked a glance over his shoulder to see how Yoshi was faring. She was fighting admirably. Most of the intelligent ninja were staying back from her, or, rather, from those deadly blades of hers. She'd already taken down five to Jamie's three.

One of the ninja slipped past his defenses and swung his blade wildly. Jamie moved his head back in time to keep from losing it, but the blade scored a hit on his right cheekbone, just below the eye. The attack threw his antagonist off balance, however, and Jamie slammed his knee into his stomach, crumpling the genin to the ground like a rag doll.

"I do not think that we can hold out much longer!" yelled Yoshi from behind him.

Just then, the familiar sound of a school bus horn sounded through the sea of black.

“We don’t have to!” exclaimed Jamie, smiling in spite of himself. “The cavalry’s coming!”

The ninja seemed to realize this, as well. Those who were closest to the two teens pressed in even harder. Those who were farther away scrambled to clear the path of the raging vehicle as it gained speed on its course of rescue.

As Jamie kicked a ninja out of his way, he caught sight of a lone ninja who was standing on the side of the warehouse farthest from the office. The figure was watching the fight with interest. Suddenly, he broke into a run toward the teens, who were still in the midst of a wave of Warui, their blades slashing left and right in an effort to clear a path to the bus.

“I hope that he does not stop!” commented Yoshi, as her swords worked in perfect harmony to disarm an opponent and deliver a knockout blow. Her back was to the lone ninja who was approaching and hadn’t seen him yet.

“That goes double for me,” replied Jamie.

Jamie saw the dragon pendant hanging from the running ninja’s neck and he realized who was leading this raiding party. He decided not to mention this one to Yoshi . . ..

* * *

“YEAH!!!” bellowed Dave as the bus scattered the outer ranks of ninja. “COMIN’ THROUGH, DUDES!”

“’*Ten and two*, Dave!’” exclaimed George from his seat behind Shawna and Amy. “’*Ten and* ***two***!’”

"Dude," the big teen called back, "don't quote the driver's manual to me. I could do this blind-folded!"

"You mean you're not already?" returned George.

One of the ninja turned to face the bus too late and ended up stuck to the front grill, his head above the hood. He was still very much alive and his eyes were windows of absolute terror.

“Doncha’ just hate hitchhikers?” muttered Dave to nobody in particular.

“We’re comin’ up on them,” exclaimed Amy. “Open the door!”

* * *

Jamie punched a ninja out of the way to clear a path to the bus. He and Yoshi ran along side of it and Yoshi jumped aboard. Jamie lunged in after her just as a shuriken bounced off the side of the bus where he’d been a second earlier. He could hear the lone ninja yelling something to the others in Japanese, but, at the moment, he didn't care to know what was said.

Jamie breathed a sigh of relief as he climbed the second step. "Nice driving," he commented. "But what about the guy plastered to the front of the bus?"

"Oh, yeah," replied Dave as he slammed his feet on the brake. Everyone aboard slammed into the cushioned back of the seat in front of them and Jamie and Yoshi were nearly knocked from their feet. As the bus came to a screeching halt, the ninja who had been stuck to the front of the bus went flying into a pile of floating tubes with an ear-piercing scream. They broke his fall, as he appeared dazed, but not dead.

Jamie had just righted himself, when Dave turned the bus left toward the road and pressed a little too hard on the gas, nearly pitching him out of the still open door. "HEY!" yelped the young ninja. He started to say something else when a black clothed arm wrapped around his neck from behind.

The young ninja's right elbow shot backward, slamming into his attacker's gut. He heard a groan and the chokehold loosened enough for him to pull free. Jamie turned to face his opponent. Some of the ninja had caught up with the bus and were climbing on it. The one who had attacked Jamie shoved forward, knocking the young hero onto his back on the steps with the genin on top of him.

"Keep driving!" ordered Jamie as he slammed the palm of his right hand into his opponent's chin. The Warui warrior groaned in pain and released his hold as Jamie followed through with a well-placed fist to the chest. He then grabbed the genin's head and slammed it into the doors, which were still open. The other ninja was now dazed enough for Jamie to push him off and out the door. He landed on the ground and rolled away from the bus.

As Jamie climbed to his feet at the base of the steps, he felt another force as a second ninja, the one with the dragon pendant, slammed into him from behind. Jamie, his patience wearing thin, refused to fall again. He put his hands down onto the top of the steps for balance and lashed out with his right foot, catching his attacker full in the face and knocking him backward. The ninja flailed wildly to regain his balance, but Jamie leaped up, grabbed the emergency handle above the door, and shot out with both feet. They connected squarely in the chest and knocked the attacker clear of the vehicle. Jamie dropped himself into a sitting position on the top step, regaining his breath as Dave closed the door.

At the back of the bus, Max Adams sat in a seat next to the emergency exit. A ninja's fist broke through the window of the door as if it were made of paper. Without a thought, the young teen climbed to his feet and grabbed the wrist, then shot out through the window with his left foot, catching its owner in the side just below the armpit. The ninja glared at him in pain, so Max repeated the action, this time releasing the arm as he did so, causing the ninja to fall from his perch to the gravel below.

A ninja dropped to the window next to the driver's seat and punched through the glass, reaching in for the big teen. Dave grabbed his assailant's wrist and squeezed until the ninja's hand was forced open. Dave glanced down and, noting an empty palm, grumbled, "Hey, dude! No token, no ride!" He yanked inward, slamming the ninja into the side of the bus to daze him then released the wrist to let the attacker fall.

* * *

The Warui party leader climbed to his feet as he watched the bus speed back toward the town. His eyes narrowed in hatred. Would he never have the opportunity to regain his lost honor?

* * *

Jamie took a sharp breath as Shawna pressed the alcohol-soaked cloth to the cut on the right side of his face. It was not as bad as he had feared, and he figured it would barely leave a scar.

“It’s already stopped bleeding,” commented the girl.

“Is the alcohol really necessary, then?” asked Jamie as he clenched his teeth for another application.

“You’ve beaten dozens of ninja,” retorted Shawna. “You don’t want to go and do something dumb and die of an infection.”

“Actually,” muttered the young chunin, “the sword hurt less than what’s on that rag.”

They both chuckled.

Yoshi sat on one of the lab tables, watching them in silence. Finally, she spoke. “Losing your touch, brother?”

Jamie cocked an eyebrow.

“See any cuts on *me*?” chided the kunoichi playfully.

Jamie knew she was just joking with him. “Sure,” he snorted, “just rub it in.”

“You sure are good with those swords.” Amy was speaking to Yoshi from her place next to Shawna on the floor.

The kunoichi smiled sadly. “Yes, I suppose that I am.”

The door to the science room opened. Dave walked in, followed by Buster and George. The big teen set a dual-deck, portable stereo down on the lab table next to Yoshi. “Forgot I had this,” he commented.

"Does the radio work?" asked Yoshi hopefully.

"I'll show ya," responded the big teen as he turned on the device and began to slowly turn the tuner. Broken sentences filled the air as he moved silently through the stations.

"Excellent!" exclaimed the kunoichi.

Dave came across a man talking. " . . . *there has been no communication from the terrorists regarding their demands and we have no way of knowing if the three people whom they were seeking ever arrived in the school. We will continue to keep you informed as updates occur.*"

Jamie sighed. "They don't know we're free."

"How could they?" inquired Shawna.

"Maybe we should bust into a house to try ta find a workin' phone," suggested Dave.

Jamie shook his head. "I'm betting the Warui planned for that and probably took out the phone lines all over town."

"You could try breaking into the *abortion clinic*," said Amy.

Buster looked at her in awe. "You can't break into . . .," his face contorted even more " . . . there's an abortion clinic in Sera?"

"Yeah," replied Shawna, "they wanted it in a bigger town, but nobody would approve it. So they came here, waived their money around, and the town council just melted in their hand."

The preacher rolled his eyes as he headed out into the hallway and toward the soda machine.

"And to add insult to injury," continued Amy, "they built it next to the First Baptist Church." She shook her head. "It's like they were rubbing it in the faces of the Fundamentalists."

Shawna looked at her cousin suspiciously.

"What?" asked Amy.

"Since when did you care about the abortion clinic?"

Amy glanced after Buster. "Since we got a cute preacher."

Yoshi chuckled.

Jamie climbed to his feet.

"Where are you going?" asked Shawna.

"I'm going to try to get some answers out of the prisoners again."

Dave scratched the stubble on his right cheek. "What makes ya think they'll be any more likely t'talk to ya now than before?"

"I don't," responded the young ninja. "But if I don't try something, I'll go stir-crazy."

Chapter Fourteen
Saturday, 2:37 PM

Donnie and Tanemura had found a roadside park at which to leave the Blazer. Donnie checked the weight of his backpack. Noticing the former Air Force sergeant grunt as he lifted it onto his back, Tanemura asked, “Is it too heavy?”

Donnie grinned at the old ninja, who was checking his ninja-to. “No more than what I wore dancing through the jungles of ‘Nam.”

Tanemura wrapped his mask around his face and tied it in place. “What do you have in your pack?”

Don checked the safety on his 12 gauge pump shotgun and replied, “Extra ammo, food, a tent, sleeping bag . . ..”

“I doubt that the latter two will be necessary,” commented the jonin, noting that they had not been forced to travel as far as they had originally planned.

“Never hurts to be prepared,” remarked the police academy teacher as he checked the doors one final time to make sure that his vehicle was locked.

They turned and stepped into the forest.

* * *

Max and Pete sat in front of the coach's office door, discussing their art. The Bluff had only two Tae Kwon Do schools, and they each happened to be in different ones.

"Actually," Max was saying, "Master Dan isn't very traditional. We don't have to learn the Korean names for the forms, or anything. Just so long as we can do them."

Pete digested the info. "Master Lee makes us remember every name, though he's a little more lenient when it comes to the other exercises."

Max chuckled. "Yeah, we do push-ups at the end of every class. He actually asked us how many we wanted to do last Tuesday. Some idiot said one."

Pete looked incredulous. "Is that all you did?"

"Don't think it was easy," commented the other. "We moved down very slowly. It took us almost a minute to do the one push-up, and a lot of us didn't finish it."

Pete appraised Max. "Did you?"

The smaller lad raised one eyebrow arrogantly. "Of course."

The double doors to the gym opened as Jamie stepped into the room. He looked in their direction and walked toward them.

"What's up?" asked Pete.

"I want to talk to the Warui chunin," was the young ninja's reply.

"What makes you think he'll be any more likely to say anything now than before?" asked Max.

"Nothing in particular," commented Jamie. "But I'm going to separate him from the others and see if that makes a difference."

The two younger boys shrugged and moved out of the way after Pete unlocked the coach's office door. Jamie turned the knob and stepped boldly inside.

The captured ninja again eyed him with intense hatred. Jamie knew that any one of these men would happily put a knife in his heart. To his surprise, the Warui chunin smiled at him in amusement.

Jamie cocked an eyebrow. "Come with me," he instructed.

The man climbed calmly to his feet and followed Jamie from the room. The two ninja walked around the stage and up to the prop room. Jamie opened the door and motioned for the other chunin to step inside, which he did without argument. The disconcerting smirk never left his face.

The prop room was a mirror image of the coach's office, at least in size and shape. Jamie pulled two large, metal prop boxes from under a shelf and sat them in the center of the room. He seated himself on one and motioned for the other ninja to do the same. The Warui ninja sat on the other box.

The two ninja regarded each other for a few moments, trying to get a feel for the other's emotions.

Finally Jamie spoke. "What's your name?"

The other warrior's face never lost that look of amusement, but he did not speak.

"You can't tell me that you don't speak English," commented the leader of Adventure. "You seemed fluent enough when we tried to interrogate you before."

"I speak English, gai-jin," remarked the other man, "but I will not give my name." His eyes narrowed. "Name's give power to those who possess them, *Jamie Raleigh*."

Now it was Jamie's turn to smirk. "And this is why you're the prisoner," he chided.

The other ninja's face darkened. "You should have killed me."

Jamie shook his head. "There are worse things than death."

"Like being held prisoner by the gai-jin student of the Funakoshi jonin."

The young hero's eyes widened in bewilderment. "Why is this so much more dishonorable than being held by anybody else?"

The other chunin's eyes narrowed in pure hatred. "You must understand how much we *loathe* you, gai-jin. Even more than any of the rest of the Funakoshi."

"Why?"

"Our war is an ancient one," commented the other ninja. "It is over four centuries old . . .."

"I'm aware of the history," interrupted Jamie impatiently.

"The point is that the rest of the Funakoshi are our enemies by birth." He leaned forward and Jamie could see the bloodlust in the man's eyes. "You *chose* to be our enemy."

Jamie's eyes narrowed. "And what I want you to understand is that I don't care about the war." He clenched his fists, glaring straight into the eyes of the Warui chunin. "I don't care about you, your clan, or *my* clan! I have only cared about four people in the Funakoshi, those being Master Tanemura, Yoshi and her parents . . . the only members who ever accepted this *westerner*!" He rose to his full height and towered over the other man, who watched him cautiously.

Jamie continued. "Because of members of your clan, two of those people are already dead." He folded his arms across his chest to fight the urge to slug the bound man. "*That's* what made me your enemy!" His eyes narrowed. "But you created an even *worse* enemy . . . not in me . . . but in Yoshika."

The other ninja said nothing.

"She would have been trained like the other women of our clan," explained Jamie. "She would have been an okay fighter, but two of you would have been able to take her. But killing her parents left her training in the hands of my master . . . and he trained her like a male in our clan." He cocked a crooked smile. "Now she's a fighting machine. And forcing her to watch you kill her parents has turned her onto *you*."

The Warui chunin remained silent.

Jamie shook his head. "You think *I'm* this *awesome* warrior?" His voice dripped with sarcasm. He was thankful that his folded arms covered his own heavy breathing. "You have more to fear in her than in any *twenty* members of our clan."

The other chunin finally averted his gaze. "Wars have casualties."

"Neither one of us wanted to be in this war!" raged the teen. "The Funakoshi just want to live their lives and forget about the past. But you won't let us!"

Jamie stepped forward and lowered his face to that of the other ninja. "Now, you've brought this on yourselves!"

* * *

Jamie sat on the cold floor of the science room, fighting tears that were trying to force themselves to surface along with one of the most painful memories of his young life. “You lost it in there, Jamie,” he muttered to himself. “You let it all get to you.”

The door to the room opened and Shawna stepped in.

Seeing her, the young ninja took a deep breath to compose himself. “What’s up?”

Shawna leaned against the wall next to Jamie and slid to the floor. “How’d it go with the other ninja?”

“I didn’t really get anything out of him,” was the response.

Shawna ran her fingers through her bleached blonde hair. “You didn’t really expect to, did you?”

Jamie sighed. “Not really.”

“Then what’s troubling you?” She gestured around at the science room and the school in general. “Other than the obvious.”

“I lost my temper.”

“Everybody does.”

Jamie brought his right hand up to rub the back of his neck. “When I looked at him, I just kept seeing those ninja who killed Yoshi’s parents.”

“Was he one of them?”

Jamie shook his head. “No.” He looked up at her. “But the guy who led the attack on their house was the same one who led the attack on us at the *Boat House*."

"Are you sure?"

The young ninja nodded. "I could never forget that man."

Shawna rested her elbow upon her right leg, propping her chin on the hand of the same arm. "Did Yoshi think it was the same guy?"

"She didn't see him," responded Jamie. "And even if she had, I'm not sure that she would have known." He looked up at the pretty honor student and explained. "Yoshi doesn't remember much of that . . . day." He sighed. "And that's a blessing."

Shawna looked into Jamie's eyes and he knew that she could see his pain. Finally, she spoke. "What happened that day?" She took her chin off her hand and used her thumb to wipe a tear from the young ninja's eye.

Jamie shuddered involuntarily as he replayed his first encounter with the Warui ninja in his mind. He had prayed she would not ask that question. Finally, he took a deep breath and said, "Our childhood ended . . .."

Chapter Fifteen
Flashback
July 24, 1988
Wednesday, 2:27 PM

A strong, chilly wind blew through the trees, uncharacteristic for the southern Missouri summers. Though not yet three o'clock in the afternoon, the sky had already darkened with thick, gray clouds that smothered the sun, which had already ceased its fighting and accepted the inevitable. A storm was coming. And it was a big one.

The four teens, three preteens and one child walked hurriedly down Poluk street, trying to get the one girl among them . . . twelve year-old Yoshi . . . home before the rain started. They had spent the past three hours practicing their martial arts in the park until the clouds had started to roll in.

The youngest three stood under the carport as Jamie, Simon, Dave and Buster walked Yoshi to the front door. "Wanna go with us again tomorrow?" asked Simon, easily as big as Dave, but much more gentle in nature.

"Weather permitting," replied the Japanese girl as she hugged each of them, lingering a moment on Jamie. "Will you call me later?" she asked him.

"Sure," he returned. "Right after supper."

She reluctantly pulled away and smiled at her friends before opening the front door and disappearing inside.

The boys regrouped by Yoshi's father's car, then headed toward Jamie and Buster's street, Speedway.

"Dude," mumbled Dave from his place next to Jamie, "do ya think she'll ever actually practice with us when we go ta the park?"

Jamie sighed. "We're probably going to have to accept that Yoshi doesn't want to be a ninja."

A slight thud from the inside of Yoshi's home, now three buildings back, caught the young ninja-in-training's attention. "Did you hear that?"

"Hear what?" asked Buster.

Jamie was already looking back toward the house curiously. "Their side window's missing its glass."

"Maybe he's fixin' it, or somethin'," suggested Zack.

"It's about to rain," Jamie pointed out. "He wouldn't have left it uncovered."

Without another word, Jamie started, at a half walk and half run, back toward the Funakoshi's house. His friends followed him.

As they approached, the young ninja-in-training heard clearly the sound of metal ringing off of metal. He'd heard this sound during his training on many occasions. Two swords, possibly more, were hitting each other.

Reaching into his pocket, Jamie produced the only real weapon that he ever carried with him . . . a *shaken*, more commonly known as a throwing star. With a trembling hand, he grasped the doorknob and pushed the door open.

From inside, he heard Yoshi's father, Kuji, yell something to her in Japanese. Though he couldn't understand what was said, the voice was filled with desperation. Jamie stepped inside, followed by his friends. They were standing inside the foyer of the house. Yoshi was standing in front of the hallway to his left, looking in terror at something out of sight. Jamie gaped in horror, as Kuji stumbled past her, three arrows protruding from his back, and his ninja-to clattering to the floor at Yoshi's feet.

The ninja master looked up at his daughter and summoned enough energy to mouth what could have only been, "Run." Then his head dropped to the floor and his eyes stared lifelessly across the room.

Through his own tears, Jamie could see Yoshi drop to her knees next to her father's lifeless form. "Father . . .," she muttered weakly. "Father . . .."

The girl had yet to acknowledge her friends' presence. Luckily, whoever had taken Kuji's life probably didn't know that they were there, either.

A man's voice came from the hallway. Jamie couldn't understand the words, but the tone was condescending. Yoshi looked up toward the voice, her eyes overflowing. Her grief turned to terror as a shadow came into view. The figure's arm reared back in preparation to throw something and the girl began to crawl desperately backward. Then the source of the shadow launched a small metallic dart at her face.

It got halfway to its target before it was knocked off course by a four-pointed throwing star. The two weapons clattered to the floor on the far side of the room.

One figure, followed by four more-each dressed from head to toe in black-stepped out of the hall, looking at the dart and star in surprise. Then the first of the assassins looked at Jamie. "Who are you?" he demanded in English with a strong Japanese accent. "How did you learn to do that?" The young ninja-in-training glanced at the speaker's neck and the dragon pendant that dangled there was forever burned in his memory.

Jamie's rage blotted out the prayer that Buster was offering to God for the death of His faithful follower. His attention focused solely upon this leader of the assassins, he replied, "I am the student of Tanemura Funakoshi."

The other four ninja gasped in astonishment, but their leader's eyes simply narrowed as he commented, "So, it would seem that the rumors are true." He gestured toward Yoshi and said, "The future jonin of the Funakoshi has been neglecting her training." He pointed to Jamie, "And the current jonin has taken a *gai-jin* as a student."

The Warui leader leaned his head back toward his followers. Almost too casually, he ordered, "Kill them."

The four genin pulled their swords and moved forward.

One took a swipe at Dave, who dodged out of the way and chided, "Hey, watch it with that thing, dude! You could put somebody's eye out!" Dave's massive fist reciprocated the attack by slamming into the warrior's face.

Dave's victim staggered backward and Simon wrapped his arms around the villain from behind. This was all that Jamie could make out before the first of the ninja got to him.

The young ninja-in-training easily dodged a downward cut. A flash of lightning illuminated the house as Jamie grabbed his attacker's wrist with his left hand and elbowed the ninja in the face with his right arm. He grimaced slightly when he felt a slight crunch.

As the shock of Jamie's attack forced the ninja to loosen his grip on the sword, Jamie grasped it with both hands and spun in a full circle, wrenching it from its owner's hands and striking the shadow-warrior down as he came back around.

Jamie looked at the man he had just killed and bile began to rise in the back of his throat. The movies had always made it seem so easy to kill someone and walk away. But the young man knew this would haunt him for the rest of his life.

Successfully fighting the urge to vomit, he looked around to see how well his friends were faring. Dave and Simon had already subdued their opponent, who was lying unconscious under an overturned bookshelf. They had gone to help Buster, who had been evenly matched with another of the ninja. Now the three were overpowering the assassin.

Jamie glanced at the ninja who Pete was fighting just as the preteen's right foot shot out, knocking the ninja backward and over Zack, who had dropped to his hands and knees behind the warrior. B.J. was watching this exchange with fascination from his spot behind the large, blue sofa.

The sound of the ninja leader's voice grabbed Jamie's attention. The words weren't aimed at him, as they were in Japanese. He looked to his right to see the ninja standing over Yoshi, whose panic-stricken eyes were glued to the man who had killed her father. Between his words, the murderer grabbed his ninja-to from its place on his back and nudged the blade belonging to Yoshi's father toward her with his foot. She picked it up and held it in an awkward defensive stance.

The ninja finished his speech and took one swipe with his sword, knocking Yoshi's blade from her grasp. The man laughed and yelled something in triumph as his blade descended toward her neck. Jamie didn't realize that the voice screaming "NOOOOO!!!" was his, nor did he remember his feet moving him to cover the distance between where he was standing and where his friend was about to die. All his awareness, and not just a slight amount of relief, was focused on the metallic sound of his ninja-to blocking that of the ninja from its mission of death.

The boy and the man locked gazes for what seemed like an eternity. Then Jamie roughly pushed his opponent straight back into the far wall, getting him as far from Yoshi as possible. Jamie's nose nearly touched the mask of the murderer as the young man proclaimed between clenched teeth, "You've taken too much here, already!"

The leader of the raiding party shoved Jamie back and then took a swipe at his head, but he easily ducked this attack. The next attack was blocked with a clang that resounded through the house. The next was blocked as well, then the next, and the next . . ..

The leading assassin couldn't get through the defenses of the young ninja-in-training. His eyes very quickly lost their arrogance as he realized that this gai-jin, who hadn't even completed his training, might be his match.

Then, his fears were proven correct. Jamie's ninja-to swung upward in an arc, neatly severing the blade of the other sword just above the hand-guard. The teen continued the momentum into a 360-degree spin and brought the heel of his left foot into the chest of the murderer, sending him sprawling from his feet.

The lead ninja looked up at Jamie, a mixture of fear and respect in his eyes. "You fight well." He produced a small, silver ball from the inside of his black vest, pushing aside the necklace to do so. "I will not underestimate you the next time that we meet." Throwing the ball, he leaped to his feet. As it hit the floor between Jamie's feet, clouds of smoke billowed forth, filling the room and blinding the young fighters.

When it cleared, the Waruiyatsu were gone.

Chapter Sixteen
November 17, 1991
Saturday, 3:02 PM

Jamie shuddered, tears running down his cheeks at the memory of that horrible day. "We found Yoshi's mother, Mai, still sitting on the couch. She never knew what hit her." He shook his head. "The things that they did to her in the instant of her death are too gruesome to talk about . . .." He cleared his throat. "We also found three of the ninja dead in the kitchen, where Kuji had fought them before Yoshi came home."

"And Yoshi tries not to remember that day because of the pain?" inquired Shawna.

"It's more painful to her because she thinks it's her fault that her father died."

"That's absurd!"

The young ninja wiped the tears from his face with his forearm. "I know. But I realize why she feels that way."

"Why?"

"Kuji was one of the finest fighters in our clan," explained the leader of Adventure. "Whenever I had the honor of sparring with him, I was usually disarmed almost immediately. He could have easily taken all of the ninja who attacked them that day." He shook his head sadly.

"But Yoshi, who *had* been neglecting her training, was his weakness. When he saw her there, vulnerable, he hesitated for just the right amount of time . . .."

"I can only imagine what she's been through."

He took a deep breath and let it out. "Yoshi's only remaining blood relative was Master Tanemura. He told her he wouldn't force her to finish her training. Not only did she choose to finish it, but she went beyond what was expected of her. Seeing her weakness in the sword as what led to her disgrace before the Warui, she bought every book that she could find on the ninja-to, and on short swords in general." He looked up at Shawna. "You've seen how good she is with two swords?" At the honor student's nod, he explained, "She taught herself that."

Shawna smiled. "Well, at least you don't have to rescue her anymore."

He chuckled mirthlessly. "She can kick my tail any day of the week now."

"Who was Simon?"

"Huh?"

"You mentioned a boy named Simon."

Jamie sighed and looked back down at his feet. "He was a friend of ours in Jameston." He shrugged. "That's a whole other story."

She nudged him playfully with her elbow. "We have nothing but time."

He smiled. "Ask me again, sometime. The memory of one life-changing failure is enough for one day."

"Okay," she responded. "No pressure."

Glancing back up at her, their eyes met. They stared at each other for what seemed like an eternity before the young ninja looked uncomfortably away and Shawna cleared her throat with the same discomfort.

"So," began the girl, "have you found any stations that play music on Dave's radio?"

Jamie shook his head. "No. All I can find are news reports about us."

"Got any tapes?"

Jamie looked toward the lab table where Dave's backpack lay. "Dave's got both our collections in his bag."

Shawna climbed to her feet and walked over to the table. After unzipping the army-green bag, she pulled out a leather tape-case. She opened it and looked inside. "'Metallica,' 'Def Leopard,' 'Poison . . .'" she looked at the young ninja, "This is Dave's case, isn't it?"

Jamie chuckled in response.

She smiled back at him and opened a smaller, red case. She fingered through it. "I don't suppose you have any *Christian* music?"

"There's a religious song on the *MC Hammer* tape," was Jamie's reply.

"I mean, do you have any tapes of only Christian music?"

The young ninja cocked an eyebrow. "Like a Gospel collection?"

Shawna sighed. "It has been a long time since you were in church, hasn't it?"

"About four years."

Shawna dug through her pocket and produced a tape that was missing its case. "Modern Christian music doesn't always sound like 'How Great Thou Art' or 'Victory in Jesus' . . . not that they are bad songs, mind you." She put the tape in the player and flipped the switch from *Radio* to *Cassette*. "Modern Christian music rivals secular rock and pop bands in quality." She pressed *Play*. The music was outstanding and sent shivers down the young warrior's back. The singer was enthralled by God. To him, God is the Creator and One Who walks with *thundering footsteps*. He is *awesome*.

Jamie walked over to stand in front of her, finding himself drawn into her brown eyes. "I thought you were all about science."

"And?" she asked.

"Can you study science and be a Christian, too?"

Shawna smiled at him. "Why would you expect me to be so unintelligent as to not see the efforts of our Creator all around us?"

* * *

Amy swore in frustration, looking off down the hallway toward where she had seen John half drag Laura. They had disappeared into the gym.

"You might want to keep your voice down when you use words like that," commented a voice from behind her with a chuckle. She turned to find Buster walking up the hallway with Dave. The preacher continued, "You might embarrass some sailor."

She flushed, though she couldn't quite understand why she felt like this around Buster . . . and only Buster. "I'm sorry," she smiled meekly. "I didn't know anybody was standing back there."

"Ease up, dude," commented Dave. "It's not like cussin's a *Bible*-bad thing."

"Actually," corrected the skinny, dark-haired kensai, "Colossians 3:8 speaks against swearing, but I'm not giving you a sermon . . ." he smiled, " . . . unless you want one."

Dave scratched his head in bewilderment at Buster's comment, then looked at the pretty girl and asked, "What's wrong, dudette?"

Amy sighed in frustration. "I just can't ignore it anymore."

Now it was Buster's turn to look bewildered. "Ignore what?"

Amy looked back down the hall. "John and Laura got into an argument over Jamie." She closed her eyes and shivered. "Laura commented on how much it bothers her that John's always harassing him. John got mad and drug her off down the hallway."

Dave and Buster exchanged worried glances. "I don't think so," muttered the big teen, as he started purposely up the hall.

Buster and Amy hurried to catch up. "Dave," said Buster quietly, "remember that we're supposed to be here to protect the students . . . not fight with them."

"I *am* protecting one of them, dude," retorted Dave.

The three pushed open the double doors to the side of the gym. Dave strode in, followed by the other two. He scanned the room. A few of the students were playing basketball, having cleared the court of the dance equipment and food. The three made their way around the stage to find the girl sitting on the floor on the side opposite the double doors. Laura's hair covered her face as she wept and there seemed to be no sign of her boyfriend.

"Are you okay?" asked Amy.

"I just . . . " she sniffled, " . . . I just need to be alone right now."

Shawna's cousin reached out with both hands and gently pushed the hair out of Laura's face. Her eye was red and was already beginning to swell.

Buster's eyes widened in horror.

Dave's heart broke. How could anyone do this to someone who seemed so sweet and innocent? "I'm gonna kill'im," proclaimed the big teen.

Buster cocked an eyebrow at his friend.

Dave sighed. "Okay. Maybe *kill*'s a strong word." He gestured at Laura. "But he does deserve what he's gonna get."

"Please," pleaded Laura, as she sprang to her feet. "Don't hurt him." She rubbed the hurt eye. "I shouldn't have provoked him."

Buster looked at her in disbelief. "Are you serious?"

"I should have known that arguing with him would just make him more angry," sobbed Laura. "I deserve what I got."

Dave had heard enough. "Listen dudette," he said, "you were the one who was right in the argument. And even if you weren't, nobody deserves to get what you did."

"Why do you stay with him?" asked Buster.

Laura sighed. "I guess it's always been tradition for the team captain of the basketball team to date the head cheerleader." Her shoulders slumped.

Amy shook her head vigorously. “He wasn’t the captain when you got together last year.” She folded her arms. “And you weren’t the head cheerleader.”

“He was cute,” she smiled meekly.

“So are Dave and Buster,” commented Shawna’s cousin, bringing a deep blush from the young preacher. “But I don’t really picture them pounding on the girls that they date.”

Laura seated herself on the floor again. “When I was picked to be the head cheerleader this year, it was a surprise.” She looked up at the three. “This is the first year that our team has ever picked someone other than a senior for the position.” She wiped the tears from her good eye and continued. “Since we'd already been together since last year, I guess, maybe, I thought it was fate.”

“What?!” demanded Buster as he crouched down next to her, followed by the other two teens. “I don’t know what god you serve, but *my* God wouldn't want you to be beaten by your boyfriend! It is not His will for us to be punching bags!”

“I . . . I just need to be alone,” muttered Laura as she climbed back to her feet and headed back toward the side doors.

Chapter Seventeen
Saturday, 3:22 PM

Jamie leaned his forehead against the cool glass of the window. He could see people moving about outside, goofing around, acting as though they were oblivious to the danger that was somewhere in this town.

Shawna was still rummaging through his tapes. "Teenage Mutant Ninja Turtles . . . Beverly Hills Cop II . . . Rocky IV . . . Top Gun . . . You have a thing for soundtracks, don't you?"

He turned around to face her. "We don't get MTV at our house, or anything, so I usually only get to hear songs in movies."

"If you don't have cable, then how do you see many movies?"

Jamie cracked a smile. "Well, once a munth, my pa and ma hitch up the horses to the wagin and we all go to the picture show . . .."

She stared at him blankly. "I'm sorry," she said finally, "I guess that was a pretty dumb question, huh?"

Jamie shook his head. "Not really. But we do have a VCR."

Shawna smiled and continued to look through his tapes.

Jamie shook his head with a grin and turned to look back out the window. He could see Buster and Dave walking with Amy across the front of the school grounds. Now that would be something. One of God's chosen ministers and the school flirt. Maybe he'd be good for her.

"Phil Collins!" exclaimed Shawna from her place at the front lab table. The young ninja turned around in time to see her pulling a tape from its case and inserting it into the tape deck of the stereo. She hit *PLAY* and, after a couple of seconds, the song *Take a Look at Me Now* began.

She approached Jamie and caught his eyes with her own. "I saved you that dance."

He blushed and smiled. "You remembered?"

She put her right arm around his waist and took his right hand with her left and said, "How could I forget?"

The two moved to the music. Shawna was a good dancer and, compared to her, Jamie felt clumsy and uncoordinated. "I'm sorry," he explained in embarrassment. "I don't dance much."

Shawna smiled at him, her brown eyes twinkling. "That's okay. Do you want me to lead?"

The young ninja nodded. "That might be a good idea."

The two of them moved around the front of the room, swaying to the music. As the seconds moved by, he found himself trapped in her gaze. Her eyes were the night sky and he could see each sparkle as if it were a star.

He hadn't realized that he was moving his face closer to hers until their lips had already met. Her left hand slipped out of his right and both her arms moved up to encircle his neck as they kissed . . ..

Chapter Eighteen
Saturday, 3:24 PM

Dave, Buster and Amy walked along the sidewalk outside the school. Dave was uncharacteristically quiet, his hands shoved into the pockets of his camouflage pants and his eyes downcast. The beauty of the twilight-cloaked, tree-covered hill that led away from the western side of the school seemed to have no effect on him.

Buster, however, was enjoying Amy's company. She was cheerful and full of life, even if she was a little too preoccupied with sex.

"So you mean to tell me that you've never . . ." she blushed, seemingly embarrassed to talk about this subject with Buster.

Buster pulled his left hand from the pocket of his black and gold windbreaker. "I don't have a ring on my hand."

"You sound like Shawna," commented Amy. "She's always talking about how sex is for marriage and shouldn't be given away so freely." She cocked an eyebrow at him. "Isn't that a little old-fashioned?"

He smiled warmly. "What's wrong with being old-fashioned?" He looked at her and said, "I just feel that there has to be something special about giving all of yourself . . . sexually speaking . . . to that special someone who God has planned for you." He shrugged. "You really can't do that if you give your virginity to someone else."

Amy cast her eyes to the ground. "I'm still a virgin."

Buster smiled. "Then why do you let your talk of sexuality mar so many of your conversations?"

She thought for a moment. "I guess it's the only way I can get attention."

Buster's eyes narrowed in confusion.

She explained. "As Shawna and I were growing up, everybody always looked at her and said 'Oh, she's so smart,' or 'Oh, she's an *Einstein*.'" She slumped her shoulders. "All I ever got was 'Why can't you be more like your cousin?'" She looked up at Buster and smiled meekly. "Problem is, I'd feel much better if I could hate her. If she were arrogant, then at least I'd see a flaw. But she treats me great. She's probably my best friend."

Buster shoved his hand back into his pocket. "And you feel that the only thing going for you is your looks."

She chuckled. "I guess *that* sounds pretty arrogant."

The kensai shook his head. "Strangely enough, you'll find that the best person for you is the one who won't be pawing you constantly."

She smiled and looked at him shyly. "Are you saying I should look for a preacher to date?"

He smiled back at her. "I think that you should accept that your emptiness can only be fulfilled properly in Jesus. Then wait for Him to send you His ideal person for you." He shrugged with a blush, "And, if that person just happens to be a preacher . . .."

"Dudes!"

Buster was startled by the big teen's first words since they'd parted company with Laura. "What?"

"DUCK!!!" Dave knocked the two of them to the ground just as an arrow whizzed by and embedded itself into a tree.

Buster looked down and realized that he had unconsciously covered Amy with his body in order to use himself as a shield for her. He blushed and asked, "Are you okay?"

She smiled at him and nodded.

He climbed to his feet, helping her do so, as well. He looked around to find a dozen black-clad warriors surrounding them. He glanced back toward the school. He couldn't even see it, as it was blocked from view by the shop building behind which they were standing. "Great, nobody can see us up here!" he grumbled as he pulled both pair of his nunchaku from their places on his belt and assumed a defensive stance.

"Dave seems happy," commented Amy, noting the smiling bloodlust that filled the larger teen's eyes.

"He just wants to take out his frustrations," muttered Buster in response. Then, to Dave, he called out, "Why don't you take up baseball card collecting?"

"Nah," responded Jamie's cousin. "I'd just as soon have the bats." He popped his knuckles in anticipation, eyeing the unmoving ninja with a wicked grin. "These dudes' heads'd make really good baseballs."

Buster risked a glance at his friend. "We need to have a talk."

Dave inhaled a deep lung-full of air, then slowly exhaled. "Ahhhhhhh . . . IT'S A GOOD DAY T'DIE!!!"

The ninja looked around, meeting each other's gazes, then one of them said to him, "It is good that you have accepted your fate."

Dave's eyes widened. "Me? I'z talkin' bout *you*, dudes." With that, his right fist shot up, slamming the ninja who'd spoken in the face and knocking him from his feet.

Buster caught a charging ninja in the gut with his right foot. As his opponent doubled over, the kensai smacked the ends of the shafts of his nunchaku into his back, knocking him to the ground. He spin-kicked another as he called out to Dave, "I don't care how much fun you think this is! We've got to get Amy to safety!"

Dave lifted a ninja over his head and fell backward into a suplex. "She'll be safe enough after we've slammed these dudes around a bit!"

Another ninja leaped at the big teen, who was still prone. He caught the Warui attacker with both of his feet and sent him flying by.

Amy screamed.

Buster turned around to see a throwing star embedded in her shoulder. She was kneeling on the ground, her teeth clenched in pain. The young kensai yelled, "She's hurt! We've got to get her out of here!"

* * *

Yoshi and George had been admiring the works in progress of the shop students. "We have a Shop Fair in the Spring every year," explained George.

Yoshi was examining what was starting to look like a table as he continued, "Sometimes, people who come to the fair buy the crafts from the students." He chuckled. "Last year, one guy built a chair with fake buffalo horns and fur all over it and sold it for five hundred dollars."

Yoshi glanced up at him and smiled. "Why didn't you take shop?"

He rolled his eyes. "They have this dumb board that you have to get current shop students to sign. You have to get twenty signatures and the students can make you do just about anything to get their signature."

Yoshi narrowed her eyes as something across the room caught her attention. “Anything?” she asked absently as she approached it.

“As long as it’s not indecent or dangerous.” He laughed. “Our freshman year, one girl had to crawl around the math classroom, cooing like a baby.”

He now noticed what she was looking at. It was a well-crafted bo staff. “Jim Chapper must have made that last year. His dad teaches karate lessons in the cafeteria twice a week. Jim graduated last year, though.”

She gently ran her hand along the carved dragons on the weapon. “It is beautiful.”

He smiled shyly. “I guess you know a lot about beauty, huh?”

She turned to him and smiled. Then, looking past him and out the window, her eyes widened. “NINJA!” She pulled her two ninja-tos from their sheaths and ran past him and out of the building.

As the door closed, he caught a glimpse of Buster and Dave fighting a dozen of the Warui warriors on the wooded hill behind the building. Amy was with them and she looked hurt. Clenching his teeth, he grabbed the staff from the rack on the wall and followed Yoshi . . ..

* * *

Buster worked his nunchaku fluidly creating a shield for his body. The ninja weren't getting through to him, but that didn't lessen his concern for Amy's safety. She sat on the ground, holding her bleeding shoulder and trusting in the big teen and the preacher to protect her. *What if it's poisoned?* He shook his head to clear it. He couldn't think about that now. He would just trust God.

A shout from the direction of the shop building pulled some of the ninja away from the two boys as the shadow-warriors moved to meet this new challenge. Buster looked to his left to see Yoshi, her twin ninja-tos working in flawless unison, cutting a path through the enemies. Following close behind was George, swinging a bo staff with practiced ease.

The young preacher looked skyward. "Lord, You are AWESOME!!!"

Yoshi performed a flip between Buster and Amy, landing to the kensai's right. "Perhaps you should pray for sword-proof hides," she suggested helpfully as she kicked a ninja.

George set himself in a crouch and caught a charging ninja with the end of the staff, flipping him effortlessly over and away from him. He then joined the defense to Buster's left, effecting a protective box around Amy.

Yoshi smashed the end of the hilt of her right ninja-to into an enemy's face as she instructed Buster, "Remind me to ask him where he learned to use that staff."

"Lord willing," replied the young kensai as he ducked a sword swipe to his head. In retaliation, he smacked the ninja in his split-toed boot with the shaft of his nunchaku, causing him to drop to the ground and cradle his injured foot.

* * *

Jamie sat on the floor of the science room, his right arm holding Shawna close. Her head rested on his shoulder.

"I can't believe that you're an uncle," she was commenting. "I thought you were an only child."

Jamie smiled. "My youngest brother is almost eleven years older than me, so I was practically raised as an only child."

"Are any of them being trained by Uncle Jamie to be little ninja?"

Jamie shook his head. "No. I don't think I'd be much of a teacher." He rubbed his eyes with his left hand, for the first time realizing just how tired he was. He continued, "Elizabeth takes tae kwon do lessons with Max Adams, but the other two aren't martial artists."

"Do they know about you?"

"That I'm a ninja?"

"Yeah."

He nodded. "They know. They're pretty good with secrets, though."

She was quiet for a moment, then said, "No pressure, but if you ever DID want to tell me about Simon . . .."

He sighed. "When we lived in Jameston, our little club was larger. We had the same people that we have now, but we also had some other friends. Four other friends, actually. There was Simon Wilson . . . the one that was with us the day Yoshi's parents were killed. There was Simon's brother, Sean. There was Mike Noddingham, who was really more Dave's friend. And then there was Ben Shalley."

"What happened to them?" asked the girl.

"Yoshi found out that Sean, Mike and Ben were selling drugs," explained the young ninja. "When we confronted them about it, they didn't deny it at all." He ran his fingers through his light brown hair. "Ben even tried to write it off as being no big deal . . . a 'natural progression' in their lives. We kicked them out of the club that day."

He leaned his head back against the wall. "I was fourteen years old and had just been accepted into the Funakoshi clan. I suppose the idea of being in a club like the one that we had started when I was nine was kind of dumb to us by then, but most of us realized that Ben's vision for our future was wrong. So Ben, Mike and Sean started a new club." He chuckled mirthlessly. "Actually it was a street gang. While Simon wasn't involved in the drugs, he was loyal to his brother, so he quit

Adventure and joined them. Even Dave's girlfriend, Tracy Bundy, joined them, causing them to break up because he took my side."

"*Your* side?"

Jamie thought back to his last summer in Jameston. "Ben wanted us to join them. He'd really thought the thing out. These kids were running through a town that never had to deal with any big crime and they caused all sorts of havoc. They were selling drugs, extorting money, organizing robberies . . . you name it, they did it." He shook his head. "I refused to join him, and all of the guys who are with me this weekend stuck with me."

"So, what happened?"

"They kept trying to provoke us." He rested his head on hers. "They wanted us to fight them pretty badly. They'd pick at us at school, home and in town. They even waited for Buster outside of his church one Sunday morning and cussed him out when he was leaving with his dad." He took a deep breath and exhaled. "That took a lot of nerve, since Buster's dad's the police chief.

"Anyway, they finally crossed the line when they lured another of our non-martial artist friends, Jack, behind the grocery store in town and beat him to a pulp." He narrowed his eyes in remembered anger. "We went after them and fought them near their meeting place in the City Park. I found out from Ben that day that the ones who had attacked Jack were supposed to have killed him. Ben was shocked when he found out they'd failed."

Shawna took his free hand in her right. "Who won the fight?"

Jamie sighed. "We survived long enough for Buster's dad to show up with a bunch of his deputies. They found a bunch of guns and drugs hidden in the dugouts of the baseball field. I guess we won, if you could call it a victory. It was hollow, though. Jack's dad left a job where he'd worked for fifteen years to move his family to Texas and get Jack as far away from all of us as he could."

"So what happened to the four who used to be in your club?"

"Simon was never really arrested, since he was basically a good person and only a *Renegade* in name."

"A *Renegade*?"

"That's what they called their gang," explained Jamie.

He continued, "Ben, Mike and Sean were sent to a juvenile detention center in the Bluff."

"Are they still there?"

"No, they've been shuffled around to different foster homes all over Missouri. I'm not sure how long this will go on, though. Dave's dad is a teacher for the Missouri Police Academy now and, as I'd mentioned, Buster's dad is the police chief in Jameston and even they couldn't find out how long the guys had been sentenced. Due to the red tape dealing with the fact that they were minors, I'm surprised we learned what we *do* know."

"Do you think they'd come after you when they get back?"

Jamie flashed another mirthless smile. "I think that's the biggest factor in my parent's decision to move here. We'd lived here from the time that I was three until I was almost eight and my parents still owned the land up here. My dad can't work anymore and they had to find a way to lower our cost of living. But they never really discussed moving back here until they found out that three very angry members of a street gang could come looking for me at any time."

Shawna returned a smile, but hers was much warmer. "I'm glad they *did* decide to move back here." She kissed him gently on the cheek, then suddenly gasped.

"What?" asked Jamie.

She was looking out the window. "I just saw a ninja outside. And it wasn't Yoshi."

Chapter Nineteen
Saturday, 3:32 PM

Yoshi grabbed the wrist of a ninja who was charging at Buster and pulled him around to face her. The warrior took a downward swipe at the kunoichi, who dodged to the side and held her opponent's blade down with her left foot as she punched him in the face, the impact of her right fist reinforced by the hilt of her ninja-to. This ninja crumpled to the ground.

"Get Amy to safety!" ordered the kunoichi as she shoved her left blade into the foot of another attacker, causing him to drop his sword and hop up and down on his good foot, howling in agony. "I am the one that they want!"

Indeed, the ninja seemed to be moving toward Yoshi as their primary target. Buster hesitated, not wanting to leave his friends in danger.

The ninja were no longer attacking him, so he quickly looked around. George parried a sword with one end of his staff, then quickly smacked his attacker across the face with the other end, while Dave kicked a ninja in the stomach, drop-elbowing him in the back of the head after he doubled over. Yoshi, as always, was fighting superbly. Her twin blades, crafted by Deck Pendragon especially for her, worked in perfect harmony, creating a whirling cyclone that thwarted attack after attack.

Buster looked down at Amy, who still sat on the ground, clutching her shoulder. The fabric of her dress was plastered to the wound with blood and the star still protruded from between her fingertips. And she was still crying. That was the hardest part. *Oh, Lord*, he prayed, *what should I do?* Then he glanced back toward the school.

And the Spiritual Anvil hit.

Somehow, they had fought their way up the hill to a point where he could see the school . . . and the path was clear for him to get Amy to safety. But how had they moved? The injured girl was still on the ground surrounded by the four teens. It was obvious that she wasn't going anywhere.

Deciding not to question God's methods, Buster reached down and gently took Amy in his arms, lifting her thin frame easily. "Keep us all safe, Lord," he whispered as he turned to leave. Then he called back to his friends, "May God guard you guys."

* * *

Max lay on the carpeted floor of the English room next to the bookshelf. Ordinarily, he hated being in this classroom. It wasn't really his favorite subject. But he was tired and, at this moment, the gray carpet felt as good as a feather bed.

The class wasn't all bad. His teacher was okay, considering the fact that she had to teach six different grade levels.

Of course, the thing he did enjoy about sixth period English was Rena Black, who was also the teacher's daughter. Every guy in the class longed to date the brown-haired, blue-eyed girl. But she had yet to choose her guy.

Also in the room lay Pete, snoring peacefully.

Wish I could sleep like he is, thought Max. Maybe being near a new person, even if he were as nice a guy as Jamie's cousin, was making him uncomfortable enough to not be able to sleep.

The tae kwon do practitioner sighed in frustration and climbed to his feet, then made his way to the door. Maybe Steve and Jeremy would let him take a nap in their room. The young teen approached the door to the hall and grasped the knob, pushing it open. To his right, the hall stretched toward the gym and the junior high classrooms. Ahead of him, another hall led toward the soda machines and the high school science room.

Steve and Jeremy were sleeping in the history room, one door to the right. He took a step in that direction and halted.

Standing halfway down the hallway was a dark-clad figure. It stood perfectly still, regarding him calmly. Then, in less time than it took for Max to blink, two throwing stars were speeding toward him.

Max dropped into the splits as the two metal stars flew harmlessly overhead. A loud CLANG rang through the hall as they struck the concrete wall behind him and he lunged back into the English room, slamming the door behind him.

The resulting noise roused Pete. “Wh . . . What?” he stammered.

“There’s a ‘non-Jamie or Yoshi’ ninja in the hall!”

Pete leaped to his feet, just as the door opened and Max was just able to stop himself from kicking his brother in the face.

“Brotherly love,” smiled Jeremy as he watched Steve’s face go pale at the barely two inch space between his nose and Max’s foot.

“Wh . . . What . . .,” began Steve, but then he just yelled, “YEEAIIEEEHHH!!!”

Max lowered his foot to the ground. “What are you doing here?” he demanded.

“We heard your door slam and got a little worried,” replied Leslie. “We heard it in my room all the way down in the junior high area.”

“There was a ninja in the hall!” growled Steve’s brother as he pulled the three visitors inside and closed the door.

“We didn’t see one,” responded Steve.

"Well . . .," countered his sibling, "I guess that's why they call ninjutsu the *Art of Invisibility.*"

At this, the window behind the teacher's desk shattered as a ninja leaped through it. Pete, closer to the window, covered his head with his arms to protect his face from flying glass. Four more ninja followed the first one into the room . . ..

* * *

"You're not going out there, are you?" demanded Shawna.

"Yes," replied Jamie simply. "Just stay here out of sight and lock the door. Don't risk looking out the door's window unless you hear three slow, knocks, followed by two quick ones." As she narrowed her eyes in confusion, he explained, "That was our secret knock when Adventure was still a club. It was the first thing that came to mind."

Shawna's eyes began to overflow. Jamie leaned in, kissing her lips affectionately. "It'll be okay." He paused. "*I'll* be okay."

As he pulled reluctantly back and opened the door, she whispered, "Be careful."

His lips parted into a smile that he hoped masked his fear. "I'm always careful."

He stepped into the hall and watched as Shawna closed the door. After he heard the CLICK of the lock, he looked through the vertical, rectangular window above the doorknob to find her staring longingly at him. He smiled weakly and turned toward the side doors of the building.

Stepping into the chill autumn wind, he shivered. How had he started to sweat?

* * *

Buster stepped up to the side door of the building. He caught a glimpse of Jamie moving around to the back of the building in the darkness. He resisted the urge to call out to him. If there were any of the Warui ninja around, he didn't want to alert them.

Amy had stopped crying, but still grunted in pain as he shifted her weight so that he could open the door. "Sorry," he whispered.

"You're forgiven," she replied. He thought that he detected a hint of a smile on her lips.

"Does it still hurt?" he asked.

"I'm trying not to think about it," was the response.

As they entered the building, the two teens heard glass shattering up the hallway to their right. "Please tell me that the nurse's office isn't in that direction," he begged.

"It's not," replied the girl. "It's in the Elementary building."

"WHAT?!"

She looked affectionately at him and added, "There's a first-aid kit in the high school principal's office."

Chapter Twenty
Saturday, 3:40 PM

Jamie moved silently up the hillside. The shadowy darkness created by the overcast sky and the looming shadows of the trees took on an almost tangible quality, as if he were in a sea of ink on the verge of drowning.

The young ninja fought hard to control his breathing. *Keep a level head, Raleigh,* he told himself. *You've never been this worked up before.* He knew he was in danger, as he had followed a shadow-warrior behind the building and heard glass breaking back here, so he realized he was probably walking into a trap.

The slightest snap of a twig caught his attention. There was someone behind him, probably ten to fifteen feet, he figured. A light crackle of dead leaves alerted him to another presence in the shadows ahead.

A chill breeze stirred and swept over the hill, catching his light brown hair as it passed. The sound of the wind dimmed as the air mass flew onward, revealing a light whirring noise. His eyes widened with sudden realization as he dodged to the right, narrowly avoiding the two throwing stars that sailed by his head from behind. A groan and the sound of something hitting the ground ahead told him where the *shaken* had gone.

Pulling a throwing dagger from its sheath on his wrist, he threw it blindly in the direction from which the stars had come. A muffled grunt told him he had hit his target, though he was less than pleased when he heard that same object fall. He ran in his opponent's direction and his heart sank as he found the ninja lying on the leave-strewn ground, his dagger having found its mark in the head, just above the right eye.

Jamie shook his head, tears beginning to run unchecked down his cheeks. "I didn't want to kill you," he murmured as another breeze rose up around him. "I never wanted to kill *anybody*." He fell to his knees on the cold earth and wept bitterly. He was so caught up in his own emotions, that he didn't even notice the broken window in the back of the building . . . or the conflict that was going on in the English room . . ..

* * *

Pete leaped over the sword that was slashing at his legs, punching his opponent in the face as he did so.

"Hey," called Jeremy playfully as he loaded an arrow, "jumping punches are illegal!"

"If you're talking about boxing, then so is this," responded Pete, leaping off the ground, spinning in place and bringing his right heel across his attacker's head.

“Honestly, Pete,” called Max as he jumped toward the wall and pushed off with his right foot, using that same foot to kick his own attacker in the chest and knocking him from his feet, “maybe we should go out for Tag Team Kick-boxing!"

An arrow whizzed by Max, taking out a charging ninja he had not seen. He whirled around to find Jeremy grinning at him.

A warrior spin-kicked Steve, knocking him over the teacher’s desk, spilling everything on the floor. The teen looked around frantically as the ninja pulled a dagger from his belt and lunged.

Steve’s right hand closed around a pair of scissors. He held them out and the attacker was unable to stop his momentum. A groan of agony escaped the cloth mask as the ninja impaled himself and died, pinning Steve to the floor.

Another warrior, apparently sensing an easy kill, drew his ninja-to and approached. Another of Jeremy’s well-placed arrows took this one down. The body landed across Steve’s first attacker, adding even more weight.

Jeremy prepared another arrow and aimed at one of the two unconscious ninja.

“What are you doing?!” demanded Max.

“Just what they were going to do to us,” responded Jeremy.

Max grasped the arrow. "No! They're beaten! We don't have to kill these two!"

Jeremy rolled his eyes and put the arrow back into his quiver.

Steve's voice came muffled from the floor. "Can somebody get these guys off of me?"

* * *

Thankfully, the office was in the opposite direction of the breaking glass. Buster sat Amy gently on the secretary's desk. He opened the first-aid kit, which was mounted on the wall over a waist-high bookshelf. After grabbing a roll of medical tape, a bandage, a piece of cloth and a bottle of alcohol, he moved back to stand in front of the girl.

He tried to examine the embedded star. The fabric of her top was glued to the skin around the wound with her blood. "I . . .," he muttered nervously, "I need to get your dress away from the wound."

She pulled a pair of scissors from the secretary's drawer and handed them to him. He cautiously cut the sleeve from the neckline to the star, then up to the inner elbow. At this, the front of her dress fell forward, revealing her undergarment. With a silent prayer for a steady hand, he focused his eyes on only the shuriken and wound, which, he was relieved to note, had stopped bleeding.

Amy grabbed the front flap of her dress and pulled it up to cover herself. "How's it look?"

"Well, the good news is threefold," explained Buster. "The arm of the star, and the wound, aren't very big." He took a breath. "The wound clotted around the star, keeping you from losing as much blood as I'd thought you had." He finally smiled. "Most importantly, the star doesn't seem to be poisoned."

"That's good," she chuckled. "And the bad news?"

His smile faded. "The removing of the star's gonna hurt. And it'll reopen the wound."

She gave him a brave smile. "I can take it."

He grasped the weapon with his thumb and index finger and looked up at her. He saw complete trust in her eyes. Still smiling, she nodded, then yelped as he yanked the star free.

He immediately put the cloth over the wound. "Apply direct pressure," he instructed her.

She released the dress flap so she could hold the cloth to the wound. Buster ignored his base instinct to gape at her, occupying himself by opening the alcohol. "You know," he commented, "despite what they show in the movies, these throwing stars are really not made to be killing weapons. Just distracting ones." He smiled, still not daring to look at her. "We're lucky for that."

He gently took her hand and the cloth away from the wound and looked her in the eye. “This is going to hurt, too.”

Her sharp intake of breath as he poured the solution on her wound told him that he had been correct. After he’d emptied half the bottle, he set it on the desk and put the bandage over the wound, securing it with the medical tape.

He drew a breath and looked up at her. She was again holding the flap up to cover herself and looking at him gently. He smiled shyly and stood up. After pulling off his black and gold *Jameston Camels* windbreaker, he draped it around her shoulders. “There,” he said. “That should keep you warm enough with your top torn.”

Her smile grew as she took his hands in hers. “Handsome *and* a gentleman,” she whispered. “A winning combination.”

* * *

Dave threw two of the unconscious ninja over his massive shoulders as Yoshi and George finished binding those who were on the ground. They’d been stripped to their underwear and gagged.

George set the last of the three dead ninja into a pile with the others. He sighed as he wiped his forehead with the back of his hand.

"The freezer's gonna be packed,"' commented Dave.

"That's gross, man," retorted George in disgust.

"Where'd ya *think* we were puttin' the dead ones, dude?" asked the big teen.

George's face paled. "I thought you were kidding!"

Yoshi, in an effort to get George's mind off the fact that their food was sharing the cafeteria's large, walk-in freezer with dead ninja, asked, "How did you learn to fight with a bo?"

Hearing Yoshi's words immediately redirected his attention. "I . . . uh . . . I had a friend in Alaska . . . where I used to live . . . before I was in the ninth grade . . . before we moved here . . .."

"Your friend taught you?" she interrupted with a smile, finding the fact that she made him tongue-tied charming.

"Uh . . . Yeah," he mumbled, rubbing the back of his neck.

"I would enjoy continuing that training," she said. Then she added, "If you are interested."

The thought of spending more time with the pretty kunoichi seemed to perk up his spirits. "Well . . . sure!"

* * *

John, Freddy and some members of the senior varsity team were taking turns shooting hoops in the gym. The team joked about Freddy's non-existent shooting ability, but he just smiled, seemingly content with being the target of this ridicule.

Their recreation was interrupted by a light voice. "John?"

The players all turned to see Laura, her hands fidgeting nervously, standing in front of the cart that held the sports equipment. One of the guys muttered, "John, you can't let your woman interrupt our practice."

John waved him off. "I'll take care of it." He headed toward Laura, irritation tangible in his gait. When he was standing in front of her, he declared, "I've told you not to interrupt me while I'm playing." He made no attempt to keep his voice down.

"You're not doing this to me anymore, John," she said, pointing at her eye.

His own eyes narrowed dangerously. "Then don't do anything wrong."

She was shaking now, though the rage in her voice made it clear that this was not from fear. "*I'm* not supposed to do anything wrong?!" Her fists clenched reflexively at her sides. "Only my parents or the law have any right to discipline me. And you're not wearing a badge, you're not my father," she yanked a ring bearing his birthstone from her finger, "and, as of right now, YOU'RE NOT MY BOYFRIEND!!!" She threw the ring at him. It bounced off his muscled chest and landed on the floor with a *clink* that could be heard throughout the now deathly quiet gym.

John's face burned red with anger. "And you couldn't have thrown your little fit when we were in private?" He took a menacing step toward her, causing her to step backward into the cart. "It's not enough that you *think* you're gonna break up with me. You also have to declare it in front of my friends?"

"I . . .," she stammered, her fear returning, "I thought that you'd control your temper in front of them."

His laughter filled the gym, but it only added to her building terror. "You think they care?" His mirth left as quickly as it had come. "The only two members of the team who would try to protect you are the preacher's kid and his friend. And they didn't come to the dance."

His hand stroked her blonde hair. "These guys are my friends. They always back me. And the only thing you've accomplished today," he now grabbed a handful of her hair, causing her to gasp in pain, "is embarrassing me! And I WON'T stand for that!"

He moved to strike her, but was caught off guard as she slammed a basketball, which she'd grabbed from the cart, into the side of his head. When he reflexively released her, she shoved it into his gut, causing him to double over. Then she burst into a run past John's stunned friends and climbed onto the bleachers, using them as steps to reach the door Dave had busted down the previous night.

As she ran, she heard John swearing at her. She risked a look back to find him leaping onto the bottom bleacher, followed by his friends. She lunged through the door, her heart pounding in her ears. Passing the empty principal's office, she kept running . . ..

* * *

As Dave, George and Yoshi approached the side doors to the school, they found Jamie, who was just coming out from behind the school.

Noticing the two ninja draped over Dave's shoulders, as well as the one George was carrying over his left, Jamie commented, "I see you ran into some, too."

"Yeah," replied Dave, "there's six more tied up in the shop building."

"How many did you encounter?" Yoshi asked her clan brother.

"Two." His face darkened. "Both dead."

She hugged him. "It is good that you are safe."

They entered the building next to the science room. Jamie did the secret knock and the door plunged open. Shawna threw her arms around him. He allowed himself to smile. Her presence made him feel better.

Dave looked at Yoshi in confusion. “Did I miss somethin’?” he asked, gesturing at the couple.

Yoshi merely shrugged.

Jamie noticed the bo staff Yoshi was carrying. Still enjoying Shawna’s embrace, he asked, “Where’d you get that?”

“It was in the Industrial Arts building,” was the kunoichi’s response. “I am going to use it to build upon training that George received in Alaska.”

Jamie looked at his clan sister’s new student in confusion. “You never mentioned that before.”

“And you never mentioned that you were a ninja,” he returned.

Jamie smiled. “Touché.”

Buster and Amy stepped, hand in hand, into the corridor. “Shawna,” Amy smiled. “I’ve got a battle scar!”

Shawna, her brown eyes widening in concern, pulled away from Jamie. “How?”

“A throwing star wound,” stated Buster. “We bandaged her shoulder, though.”

“Dude,” muttered Dave. “I just wanted to apologize. If I hadn’t been so caught up in poundin' on the ninja, she wouldn't of gotten hurt."

Amy smiled. "I'm still alive. You're forgiven."

Suddenly, Laura burst into the hallway, coming to a stop right in front of Dave, who unceremoniously dumped his two prisoners to the floor. "Laura?" he asked, noticing the panic in her tear-filled eyes. "What's wrong?"

She looked at him for just an instant before throwing herself into his arms. "Dave," she cried, "please help me!"

John Bowers ran into the hall, followed by Freddy Jenks and four other teens. Seeing Lauraa and Dave, the jock raged, "This isn't your business!"

"It looks like she just made it his business," said Shawna, her eyes staring daggers at the basketball player.

"LEAVE ME ALONE!!!" screamed Laura as she moved behind Dave, who stood before her protectively.

By now, a crowd, which included the rest of Adventure, had begun to form up the hallway, just outside the English room.

"She hit me with a basketball!" roared John, pointing at the lump that was growing on the side of his head.

"Dude," thundered Dave. "After what you've done t'her, I wouldn't pity you if she'd run over you with a bus!"

"Get outta my way!" John took a swing at Dave, who caught his wrist, twisted his arm behind his back and slammed him against a soda machine.

"Listen up, dude," commanded Jamie's larger cousin menacingly. "She's made her choice. She doesn't wanna be with a girl-beatin' dog-lunch like you. So just leave it alone!"

Freddy took a step forward, but stopped when Yoshi's hand shot up and grasped his throat. "You were not thinking of interfering, were you?" she asked sweetly.

He shook his head, his eyes wide with fright.

She squeezed a little. "Good." Then she released him.

Dave pulled John back from the soda machine and shoved him in the direction of the basketball players. "Now, fer yer own safety, I'd put as much distance between you and me as possible . . . if I wuz you."

John glared past Dave at Laura. "Dave won't be here forever."

Jamie stepped forward. "But I will be." Everyone now stared at the young ninja. "She's taking the road that leads away from you, Bowers.

And she'll always have someone there to protect her from you."

The jocks and their puppet turned and stormed away.

Laura threw her arms around Dave and sobbed into his Hawaiian shirt. Dave wrapped his own arms around her comfortingly. "'S'okay, dudette. He'll never hurt you again."

Jamie's own mouth turned into a slight smile. He had never seen Dave this gentle. It was as if he were afraid that he might break the small cheerleader.

* * *

John, Freddy and their friends sulked on the bleachers. The team captain spun a basketball between his hands. Nobody had spoken since the confrontation in the hall.

Finally, John leapt to his feet and threw the ball to the floor with such force, the sound reverberated throughout the gym. "How DARE she!!!"

His friends looked up at him, not really shocked by the outburst. "She wants to break up with me? FINE!!!" He kicked a bleacher as he said the last word. This caused another echo throughout the gymnasium. "I can have any girl I want!"

"Then why be mad?" asked one of the players, a curly-haired teen named Jarod.

John thought for a moment. "I don't want *Dave* to have'er." John burned with anger at the thought of Laura in the arms of Jamie's cousin. She belonged to *him*. SHE WAS HIS PROPERTY!!!

He crossed his arms and looked sullenly in the direction of the coach's office. Jamie and George had just finished locking several more prisoners in there.

An idea formed in his mind as he looked at the unguarded door to the makeshift jail. A dark smile played at the corners of his mouth. He had a means to get even. Shawna had planted the seeds of rebellion by constantly bad-mouthing him to Laura. Jamie had brought his lumbering bear of a cousin to the school. But, most importantly, Dave had stolen his property.

He grinned as he fidgeted with the keys in his pocket . . . keys to which the coach would only have entrusted his star player. He would get even . . ..

Chapter Twenty-One
Saturday, 9:30 PM

Laura calmed down enough to explain what had happened in the gym. All of Adventure, as well as Jamie's local friends, had gotten a good chuckle at her improvisation and Jamie hadn't missed the irony of her weapon choice.

The group spent the next few hours visiting in the science room, each taking turns monitoring the halls and discussing ideas for escape. The rest of the students were getting restless and Jamie feared a breakdown of order if they did not find some way to contact the outside world.

As they noted the hour, everyone began to file out of the room. They needed rest before they could think through any ideas. Max and Pete would sleep in Steve and Jeremy's room, since the English room was missing the glass in one of its windows.

"Ya want me to sleep outside'o yer room?" Dave asked Laura. "Just in case yer *ex* pays a late night visit?"

She smiled shyly. "That's sweet. But he wouldn't dare try anything with you in the building."

Dave cleared his throat. "Maybe I'll just walk ya to yer room, t'be safe."

After Amy had given Buster a quick kiss on his cheek, causing him to turn three shades of red, Laura accompanied Shawna's cousin and Dave from the room and headed toward the stairs. They were sleeping in the typing room with Shawna, who stayed behind to wish Jamie a good night.

As she watched Dave and Laura leave the room, Shawna's smile nearly took in both ears.

"You look happy," commented Jamie.

"She's my best friend," stated the girl wistfully. "I've always wanted her to leave him." She looked up at the young ninja, tears of joy overflowing. "Look what it took. The Lord uses even the strangest situations to do good."

"Amen," Buster agreed.

"When I was gone last year, Laura drove all the way to Aurthur to see me everyday."

"Aurthur?" asked Yoshi.

"I was arguing with my mother a lot last year, after my grandfather . . . her father . . . died," explained Shawna. "We were just irritating each other. So I went into foster care."

Yoshi's confusion was obvious. "Why did I not see you at school?"

Shawna wiped the tears from her eyes. "To keep from messing up my grade-point average, I stayed enrolled here. Laura and Amy brought me my homework and my foster mother home-schooled me."

"I'd always wondered . . .," mumbled Jamie.

Shawna wrapped her arms around his waist. Kissing his lips, she said, "You've bared your heart to me this weekend, Jamie Raleigh. It's only fair that I do the same."

* * *

Donnie grunted under the weight of his backpack. "You easily had as much stuff as I did. Why isn't it slowing you down?"

Tanemura grinned as he leaped over a fallen log. "My backpack isn't as large as yours."

Dave's father, struggling to keep up, examined the wiry, older man. "Where'd you put everything?"

Tanemura turned around. His mask covered his mouth, but Don could see a smiling twinkle in his eye as he replied, "*That* is a trade secret."

The two had been traveling for hours. As tired as they were, they didn't want to stop to make camp, feeling that they must be getting close to the town. "How much farther, you think?" asked Donnie.

Tanemura stopped for the first time in two hours, not at all winded, and looked around. "I have never been through these woods before, but . . . " he pushed up the sleeve of his wrist gauntlet to see his watch . . . "I would say another three hours, or so."

Donnie's groan made the old jonin chuckle as they continued onward.

* * *

Unseen by anyone in the dark, chilly Missouri night, several dark figures climbed, one at a time, from a second floor window of the high school building. The final three carried an unconscious form each. They descended silently to the hill behind the two-story structure, then vanished into the darkness . . ..

* * *

Jamie had just felt sleep begin to overtake him, when he felt himself shaken violently. "Jamie!" a familiar, feminine voice called urgently.

"Wh . . . what?" mumbled the leader of Adventure as he opened his eyes and Yoshi slowly came into focus.

"You must come at once!" She tugged him into a sitting position.

He climbed unsteadily to his feet. His contact lenses were soaking, so he grabbed his glasses from one of the lab tables.

"Whassup?" grumbled Dave.

The kunoichi's face darkened. "The prisoners are gone."

* * *

Dave swore. The door to the coach's office was standing open. There was no sign of it having been forced open. "Are ya sure you an' George *locked* it?"

Jamie cocked an eyebrow. "Of course."

The big teen ran his fingers through the brown curls on top of his head. "Who had the key?"

"I had it," responded Yoshi. "I was just coming to check on them."

Buster scratched the stubble forming on his chin from two days without shaving. "Does anyone else have a key?"

Jamie shrugged. "You mean, other than the coach?"

George ran through the side doors to the gym and skidded to a stop next to Yoshi. Looking into the coach's office, he exclaimed, "Our escaped prisoners have prisoners!"

* * *

Dave swore loudly, his curses echoing through the upstairs hallway along with the sound of his open palm striking the chalkboard of the typing room. The classroom was in disarray. Desks were overturned, typewriters broken and the monitor for the teacher's computer was lying on the floor, its screen caved in.

Jamie trembled, icy fear gripping his heart. They'd taken Shawna, Laura and Amy. Why those three, in a hallway full of classrooms filled with potential hostages?

There was a note on the blackboard that was written in Japanese. Yoshi was reading it. "They are going to return tomorrow morning at dawn." She looked at her clan brother. "They want us to be ready to fight them."

"Why don't they just ask for our surrender?" wondered Buster aloud.

"We have disgraced them," explained the kunoichi. "For them, defeating us in combat will restore their loss of honor."

Jamie noticed a book lying on the floor. He fought back his fear for the girls' safety as he bent down and picked it up. The maroon, faux leather cover read *The Holy Bible*. Opening it, he read the words on the inside front cover:

Shawna,

It's been fun having you here. Be sure to come and visit me. You've been an awesome foster-sister.

Love,

Alexandria

He didn't recognize the author of the note. If Shawna survived this, maybe he'd get a chance to ask her.

NO! he thought angrily to himself. *We'll get through this!* "If they want a fight," he spoke aloud, catching his four friends off guard, "we'll GIVE them a fight!"

"My brother," Yoshi commented with concern, "calm yourself. We will be of no help to them if we cannot keep level heads."

The young ninja felt a sudden flush of remorse. His shoulders slumped and he said, "This is all my fault."

Buster put a comforting hand on his teacher's shoulder. "No, it isn't."

Jamie's eyes looked up to catch those of Adventure's preacher. "How can you be so calm?"

"Yeah, dude," muttered Dave. "We've seen how you and Amy look at each other."

George added, "She was always flirting with guys, but I've never seen her look at someone like she looked at you."

Buster took a moment to gather his thoughts. "She was desperate for a guy who would look past her body to see her heart. It's even more beautiful." He looked skyward. "But I'll pray . . .

and I know that the Lord will keep watch over them. We just have to have faith."

Suddenly, John burst into the room, followed by a panting Freddy. "Where's Laura?" demanded the jock.

"Yer bein' here just puts me in that much worse of a mood," grumbled Dave as he took a menacing step toward them.

Buster stepped between them. "Dave," he pleaded, "be calm. Beating the soup out of John isn't going to bring her back."

"It'll make me feel a lot better," grunted the big teen.

"What are you talking about?" asked John, his eyes wide in panic. "What'd they do?"

"What did *who* do?" asked Yoshi, her eyes narrowing in suspicion.

John and Freddy looked at one another in fear. "Uh . . .," they stammered in unison.

The kunoichi leaped over a desk and grabbed John, shoving him back against a wall. Freddy started to move toward them, but a glare from the girl made him think twice.

If Jamie hadn't been so shocked, he might have laughed. The sight of the smaller Japanese girl holding the tall boy against a wall was quite funny.

Her right arm crossing his chest, holding him in place and her eyes locked on his, Yoshi's left hand shot into and out of the front pocket of his pants like lightning. The others almost didn't even see her move. Then she shoved him away from her.

As the jock slammed into a bookshelf, Yoshi ordered, "Do not move." She opened her left hand to reveal what she'd taken from him . . . a set of keys that were attached to a basketball-shaped key-chain. She flipped through each of them until one caught her eye. Pulling another key from a pocket in her vest, she compared them.

"A match," she sighed, handing both to Jamie. "Here is our traitor."

Jamie glared at John. "I guess it makes sense that the coach would give a key to his favorite player."

"I should pound you into putty, dude," rumbled Dave.

"Don't bother," interjected George. "He's already done enough damage to himself." He followed Yoshi, who was still staring daggers at John, out the door.

Buster followed them, pausing to give the jock a look of pity. He continued George's thought. "That popularity that he's so proud of is going to end when everyone finds out how much danger they were in because of his need for revenge." He shook his head sadly and walked out of the room.

Dave glared at him as he walked by, causing John to wince in fear. The big teen, obviously fighting to control himself, clenched his fists at his sides and the popping of each of his knuckles was clearly audible in the dead quiet of the room. Still shaking in barely contained rage, he walked out the door.

Jamie walked by, not even stopping as he tossed John's keys at the jock, who was too scared to even raise his arms to catch them. They bounced off of his chest and jingled as they hit the floor.

Bowers and Jenks were left to look about the trashed room and to reflect upon the results of their actions.

* * *

Jamie opened his eyes. Meditation wasn't working. Dave had finally drifted off, after an hour of growling about creative ways to torture John Bowers. But Jamie couldn't sleep. He was too wired.

He had considered gathering the students and leading them through the woods on the southern part of town with the intention of reaching the next town that way. But the ninja were trained to not be seen. A forest would be an easy place for the Warui to hide and would be a bloodbath for the students. No, meeting them at dawn seemed to be the only thing to do at this point.

The clock that hung over the science room's chalkboard clicked on the third hour as he watched it. He sighed. Maybe if he hadn't admitted to Shawna his feelings . . . if he hadn't kissed her . . . then they might not have taken her.

He pulled one of the metal chairs out from the front lab table and seated himself. Maybe they should have killed the captured Warui ninja. It would have freed the students from the fear that the ninja could escape. It would have meant that Shawna would still be with him.

He looked at her Bible, which lay open upon the lab table before him. The young ninja had been flipping through it, reading her notes. He picked it up and read the only note in the margins of a particular page in the Book of Matthew, catching his interest by being dated two days previous:

Led during prayer to outline this verse.

Part of a single verse, 16:26, was carefully highlighted in yellow. It read:

"For what is a man profited, if he shall gain the whole world, and lose his own soul?"

Jamie blinked in amazement. It was as if God was, through Shawna's outline of this verse, refuting the young ninja's chain of thought.

He set the Bible down and looked up. All he saw was the ceiling. But he wasn't expecting to see the Physical Manifestation of the Sovereign Creator of the Universe, anyway. "God," he began, "I know you're there. I guess I've always known. I knew it when I went to the altar when I was twelve and I knew it when my mom and I stopped going to church. I've known it every time I've glanced over the spine of my Bible, which I haven't even pulled off the bookshelf in something like three years."

He sniffed and wiped his eyes with his hands. "Buster, Shawna and Master Tanemura are so confident in what they have with You. I want what they have." He lowered his eyes to the floor. "So, here I am God. I've ignored You since I was thirteen years-old. How can You ever forgive me for *that*?" He was crying now, shaking slightly as the tears flowed.

I JUST CAN. He opened his eyes with a start. It had been a small voice, not audible to his ears. But his heart, the part of him with which God was most concerned, had heard it quite clearly.

He smiled, wiping the tears from his face. "Thank You," he whispered.

Chapter Twenty-Two
Sunday, 5:12 AM

Don could only shake his head in awe. It was one thing for Dave's forty year-old father to be in good shape. He worked in law enforcement, after all. But Tanemura was at least thirty years his senior and seemed to be moving through the forest without breaking a sweat.

The former Air Force sergeant had spent most of the night swearing at the weather. The thick clouds had completely covered the moon, causing them to have to use flashlights to see, which made them stand out like the proverbial sore thumb. However, they had been using them for many hours and there hadn't been any incidents.

Ahead, the Funakoshi jonin stopped. Donnie hurried forward to see what was happening. He was thrilled to see houses and streetlamps. When he glanced at Tanemura, however, his elation turned to dread. The older man's eyes were sweeping the darkness ahead. He had also stopped breathing.

"What is it?" whispered Donnie.

At that, Tanemura's hand shot out, catching an arrow that had been intended for the policeman's temple.

To Donnie's credit, the seasoned veteran did not flinch. His eyes narrowed at the shadows running silently through the trees. It had been years since he had seen mass combat but the old training was still in him. The silence of the early morning darkness was broken only by the pumping of his shotgun.

A battle cry in Japanese sounded from a tree overhead as a figure dropped at the two men, light from a nearby streetlamp reflecting off its drawn blade. A shot blasted out from Donnie's gun and the attacking ninja was dead before it hit the ground.

Six of the shadow warriors charged out of the trees, their own swords drawn. Donnie was acutely aware of the smooth scraping sound of Tanemura's ninja-to drawing from its sheath at his side.

The two men, ninja and soldier, instinctively moved back-to-back. "How many back there, old-timer?" asked Donnie casually.

"Eight," responded Tanemura. "And on your side?"

"Six." He pumped his shotgun again. "They must have been expecting you to be alone."

"This is merely a surveillance party," responded Tanemura. "They were not expecting me to come this way at all."

One of the eight ninja on Tanemura's side broke rank and charged the old jonin. An overhead strike was blocked by Tanemura's blade, which then swiped at the ninja's midsection, felling the shadow warrior.

Two more charged at him. He dodged one attack and blocked another, grasping the wrist of the first attacker and shoving that one's blade into the gut of the second. He then kneed the first one in the stomach and, when he doubled over, slammed the hilt of his own sword into the back of the first attacker's neck, sending him into unconsciousness.

Donnie had seen none of this, his eyes focusing on his own six ninja. "You're down to five, aren't you?" he said to Tanemura.

"It will soon be four," responded the older man.

The six on Donnie's side eyed him warily. "Why aren't mine attacking yet?"

"They have heard of me," responded Tanemura. "They know what to expect. They know of my abilities. But you are . . . what do you American's call it . . . a wild card?"

Donnie took a deep breath and then released it. "Well, then, aces are high!" His outburst seemed to draw the ninja out of their contemplation and three of them charged him. He blasted one of them, then blocked the downward strike of another one with his gun as he kicked that one in the groin, causing him to drop to his knees in agony. Then he slammed his fist into the face of the third one, his blow augmented by the hardness of the stock in his hand. This one was knocked back a few steps, giving Donnie just enough time to cock the gun again and take him out with another shot.

The fourth ninja threw a silver ball at the ground between himself and Donnie. The veteran aimed his weapon at the center of the cloud and fired. A groan escaped and, when the smoke cleared, that ninja was laying in a pool of his own blood. "Don't know why he thought that'd work," muttered Donnie.

Two of the ninja facing Tanemura moved to either side in front of them. The old man eyed each of them, unable to suppress a smile. Then he dropped to the ground, rolling between them as they swiped at him but only hit air. As he rolled back to his feet, he found that another one had moved in so that he was surrounded by the three of them.

The one to the right charged him, only to be disarmed by a kick to the hand. The sword flew several feet away and landed silently on the leaf-strewn ground. A spin kick from the jonin sent its owner to join it.

The one to his left swiped at his neck but he ducked it, swiping the Warui ninja's legs with his own sword. The warrior dropped to the ground, howling in agony.

The one in front of him moved up and attacked him. Tanemura blocked attack after attack, not bothering to reciprocate. The Warui ninja glared at him in rage, only to be angered even more by the smile in the Funakoshi jonin's eyes.

The antagonist growled as he thrust his blade out wildly, only to have Tanemura move to the side and catch him in a bear hug, pinning his arms to his side.

"'Say goodnight, Gracie,'" chuckled Tanemura.

The attacking ninja, who obviously did not speak English, glanced back at him in fearful confusion.

Tanemura's knee shot up, kicking the other ninja in the back, striking a pressure point that caused the Warui to empty the contents of his bladder. Then the old ninja released him and chopped him in the back of the neck with the edge of his hand, knocking him senseless.

Donnie dropped his empty shotgun, pulling the pistol from its holster on his belt. Before he could aim it, another of the ninja was on him. He moved forward, bringing his left arm up and blocking the wrist of the hand that was holding the ninja-to. He shoved that warrior back a few steps and the veteran's left foot shot up, catching the ninja in the chin and knocking him from his feet. Holding his foot aloft, he reached out with his right hand and grabbed the boot knife that was sheathed there, pulling it free. He dropped his foot into a step toward the last of the six ninja and threw the knife, catching the warrior in the chest and sending him to the ground.

The ninja who had just been kicked in the chin leapt to his feet, but a well aimed shot from Donnie's pistol took him out.

He looked around at his fallen enemies. "*That* was a workout!"

Tanemura knocked a throwing star out of the air with a swipe of his sword. Spinning around, he hurled his ninja-to at the ninja who had thrown it. Not expecting an attack of this nature, the ninja clumsily blocked it, taking his eyes off of Tanemura just long enough for the ninja master to close the distance between them and kick the other ninja in the chest with a flying side kick. He was sent sprawling from his feet as Tanemura snatched his own ninja-to from the ground and swiped outward to his left, taking out the final ninja, who was moving in to attack.

The ninja who had just been knocked down started to rise. A gunshot rang out and his head snapped to the side, dropping him instantly.

Tanemura turned to see Donnie standing over a ninja who was holding his own groin, tears running from his eyes. Donnie's pistol was aiming at the prone warrior, but the soldier's eyes were on Tanemura. "I didn't do that," he said in confusion.

"DROP YOUR WEAPONS!!!" called a voice from behind one of the buildings. Twenty camouflage-wearing men with machine guns ran out of three houses, surrounding them and leveling their weapons.

Don and Tanemura exchanged looks . . . Don's irritated and Tanemura's incredibly calm . . . as they threw their visible weapons to the ground and raised their hands in defeat.

"I wonder if they saw the whole fight before they decided to come out or if they slept through most of it?" grumbled Dave's father.

One of the soldiers stepped forward and, after squawking "We've caught some of the ninjas" into his two-way radio, pulled the mask from Tanemura's head. All of the soldiers, as well as Don, were unnerved by the Japanese man's smile.

"Are you taking us to your commanding officer?" asked the old ninja.

"You'll see the colonel soon enough," was the response from the man who had removed the mask.

Tanemura's smile widened. "Now we are getting somewhere."

Chapter Twenty-Three
Flashback
August 10, 1988
Saturday, 7:30 PM

Jamie fastened the *tabi* on his feet. The split-toed boots always felt less than comfortable. They made it feel as if his sock were bunched up between his big and second toes.

He glanced to the table at his side. The mask of his suit lay upon it, its blackness marred here and there by specks of dust that had landed on it in the short time it had been there. He was puzzled by the fact that Tanemura had insisted he wear an actual ninja suit for the test. It was not something that was typically allowed for a student to wear.

He reached out and grabbed the cool cloth, pulling it over his head. He wondered briefly if this was how Peter Parker felt when he wore his mask. Of course, his favorite superhero's mask covered his eyes. The ninja mask did not do that for Jamie. Those who were testing him would be able to see the fear in his eyes.

He took a deep breath, somewhat uncomfortable with the way the air came through the material.

His right hand moved up to grasp the cool hilt of the ninja-to that was strapped to his back. He pulled it from its scabbard and ran his left thumb along the edge of the blade. The aluminum felt smooth, but not sharp.

A knock at the door caused the young ninja-in-training to jump, nearly dropping the weapon. He nervously slid it back into its sheath and said, "Yes?"

"Are you decent?" called Yoshi's voice.

"Yeah," replied Jamie.

The door opened and his clan-sister peered in. "They are ready for you."

* * *

Jamie stood with Yoshi, one elder and a group of ten uniformed ninja at the gate to the City Park. He glanced back at the travel trailer where he had gotten ready, wishing he could run back in and hide.

The elder . . . Tatsu, if Jamie remembered correctly . . . handed him a pair of goggles. "These are to protect your eyes." He picked up a belt and handed it to Jamie, then pulled Jamie's sword from its sheath. "The weapons in the pouches on this belt are coated in a washable, white ink of a type that will show up on black fabric." Another Japanese man handed Tatsu a flask of yellow liquid, which he promptly poured into Jamie's scabbard. He then replaced Jamie's blade. "The ninja who are testing you have been instructed that they are *dead* when you hit them with one of your weapons and leave a white or yellow mark upon them."

The elder gestured to one of the ninja who was dressed in his black suit, whose eyes Jamie recognized as those of Tang Shakato—a member of a family who frowned upon Jamie being trained by Tanemura, and said, "They each have green ink of a type that will show up on the black fabric of your suit."

The old man gestured toward the interior of the park. "Your sensei and the remainder of the elders are waiting for you in one of the dugouts in the baseball field. To pass the test, you merely have to get to them." He narrowed his eyes coldly at the teen. "One green mark and you fail."

Tatsu and the other ninja disappeared into the park. "Great," mumbled Jamie, "my favorite color is going to make me fail."

Yoshi stepped up to him and grasped one flap of his vest, pulling it open and stuffing a white cloth into one of the inner pockets.

"What's this for?" he asked.

The girl smiled at him and he was caught off-guard by just how beautiful a sight it was. "In the Middle-ages, did the princess not give a white handkerchief to her champion?"

"I'd hardly say I'm a champion," was his response.

She wrapped her arms around his neck and kissed him lightly on the cheek. Even through the material of the mask, her lips felt warm. "You *are* my champion." She looked into his eyes and his breath caught in his throat. "Be careful." She then pulled away and disappeared into the park.

Jamie looked after her, his eyes narrowed in confusion. Their friendship had strayed to such an affectionate level once before and they had both decided that it should never go there again.

Or had they?

The young man shook his head to clear it. He had to keep his mind focused on the task at hand. The baseball field was only a few hundred feet inside the park but, with a clan of ninja between him and that destination, it might as well be several hundred miles. He inhaled deeply, held it for a few seconds, and then let it out as he took a step toward the gate. He then took another. Then another. Until, finally, he was inside.

The trees cast long shadows in the twilight. The shadows cast by some looked as if they had claws and were reaching for him. The ninja-in-training closed his eyes, willing himself to tune out his vision. In this light, he knew his sight could only hinder him.

As he stopped paying attention to his eyes, his other senses began to sharpen. The smell of the grass . . . the feel of the cool air on what little of his skin was uncovered . . ..

. . . the whirring sound of something that was flying toward him.

Jamie dropped to the ground and rolled as two rubber shuriken flew over his head in different directions. He sprang to his feet and darted toward a tree. A black-clothed figure leaped out and launched another green-painted star at him. His blade leaped from its scabbard and swatted it away and then doubled back to swipe at the attacker's midsection, leaving a trail of yellow.

The warrior groaned in frustration and moved aside.

The teen moved past the tree and ninja, running toward the baseball field.

Another warrior jumped from a bush and swung a green-tinted bo staff at him. Jamie barely ducked the staff. *It's obvious that these guys don't want me to finish this test*, he thought as he leaped over an attempt to trip him with the weapon. *They could at least play a little less roughly.* At the height of his leap, the teen lashed out with his right foot, catching the ninja in the chest and sending him to the ground.

Another swipe of Jamie's ninja-to left a trail of yellow running diagonally down the prone warrior's vest.

He ran past and reached the baseball field. On the side opposite him, he could see Yoshi and the elders, who had now noticed him. Fearing that the ink on his sword might dry, he sheathed it, and then started walking warily toward the dugout.

His heart leaped into this throat when he heard the yell. Since it was in Japanese, he had no idea what was being said, but it did alert him to the fact that the other dugout was occupied as well.

He broke into a run toward the elders as he reached into a pouch on his belt, producing five plastic, white-coated shuriken. He could see the eight remaining ninja who had gone into the park pouring out of the Visitor's dugout.

Three of the five shuriken reached their targets. The other five ninja were still running on an interception course with him. He leaped to the ground and rolled through them as their ninja-tos swung harmlessly at air.

When he had finished the roll, he was back on his feet and he pulled own blade from its scabbard, taking out two of his opponents with one swipe. Another ninja took a swipe at Jamie's head, while a second attempted a swipe at his feet. Jamie ducked the head shot, blocking the other shot with his own sword. His blade slid up that of the blocked warrior, slicing across both of his forearms and leaving a trail of yellow there.

That ninja yelled something in Japanese and threw his weapon to the ground in disgust.

Jamie dodged to the side as the ninja who had attacked his head attempted a downward swipe of his blade. Jamie's own weapon swept in an upward arc, leaving the ink on the warrior's face.

He had one opponent left. And he could now tell that it was Tang. The two of them circled each other warily. The green ink on the blade of Tang's sword glinted in the evening light.

And then he was striking, pressing forward viciously. Jamie could do nothing but block the attacks, each strike of metal on metal rattling his teeth. Whatever the reason for this test, it was obvious Tang did not want him to pass it.

In desperation, Jamie used the split toe of his right boot to catch some of the dirt of the field. As he blocked an attack, he lashed upward with that foot, kicking Tang in the face and releasing a cloud of dust that caught the ninja off guard.

Jamie swatted the green inked blade away from its wielder. Then his own yellow mark was on the stomach of Tang's vest.

The ninja glared at Jamie with barely controlled rage.

"He has beaten you, Tang," called one of the elders from the dugout. "Let him pass."

Obviously using every ounce of self-control he had, Tang moved to the side and Jamie walked the remaining ten feet to the dugout and dropped inside.

The elders examined him. "There is not a green mark on him," one of them said in awe.

Tanemura stepped forward and bowed to his student, who returned the act of respect. "You have done well, my pupil."

"Thank you, sensei." Jamie risked a glance at Tang, who had removed his mask, his hate-filled face now regarding the teen coldly.

"You were obviously not exaggerating, Tanemura," commented Tatsu. "He is quite skilled."

Jamie blushed at the attention as he removed the goggles and his mask. "I was lucky."

Tanemura shook his head. "None of the ninja who tested you today wanted you to complete this test. They fought with every ounce of misguided disdain for you that they have." He smiled. "You have surpassed my every expectation."

Another elder, this one a woman, came forward with a wooden box. Tanemura opened it and produced a necklace with a small sparrow pendent dangling from the silver chain. "Jamie Raleigh," he said as he placed the chain over his student's head, letting it fall into place around his neck, "it is with great honor and pride that I admit you as a chunin to the Funakoshi ninja clan."

Jamie's eyes shot up at his sensei. Had he heard correctly? "What?!"

"You are now a ninja," commented Tatsu.

Jamie's eyes moved back and forth between the two older ninja in confusion. "But, I . . . I . . . I'm only fourteen!"

"And already as skilled as many of our adults," said Tanemura, looking around to regard the ninja Jamie had defeated to get to the dugout.

"But remember, young ninja," cautioned Tatsu, his face softer than before, "your training will *never* be 'complete.' Everything that you do in life will be a learning experience. Just as helping your sensei to complete Yoshika's training will be."

A gentle brush of a hand on Jamie's shoulder brought Jamie's attention to Yoshi, who smiled up at him and embraced him. He gladly hugged her back as she whispered in his ear, "You are *my* champion."

Chapter Twenty-Four
November 18, 1991
Sunday, 5:35 AM

Jamie awoke to gentle hands shaking him. He opened his eyes to find Buster and Yoshi standing over him. All the members of Adventure were present, along with George, Steve, Max, Jeremy and Leslie. Jeremy could never sleep past dawn, so they had used him as an alarm clock this morning.

"Nice pillow," commented Buster with a smile, gesturing to the open Bible on the table in front of him. Jamie had read everything on the page with the outlined verse before dozing off.

His dreams had taken him back to the day that his skill, when fighting the Warui ninja who had killed Yoshi's parents, had prompted the Funakoshi to test him early. He would have much rather had Mai and Kuji safe and alive with Yoshi than to be a fourteen-year-old ninja.

He sighed and rubbed his eyes, fighting back the emotion of that time in his life. He looked out the window to see it was still dark. The clock read 5:35. He'd gotten less than three hours of sleep--bent over a lab table--but he felt surprisingly refreshed.

"We're all ready, dude," said Dave.

Jamie gave him an irritated glance. "What do you mean by 'we're all?'"

"We're ready to fight with you," stated Pete.

"Hold on," snapped their leader. "They only want Yoshi and me."

"That is what I have been trying to tell them," stated Yoshi. "But they are ever so stubborn."

Buster's face was a mask of determination. "We started this together. By the Grace of God, let's finish it together."

Jamie looked at the young preacher and thought back two nights, to the prayer his friend had offered. He had called them a family. And he was right. They all cared very deeply for one another and had put their lives on the line for each other. If anything, this weekend had served to strengthen that bond.

"And what about our new members?" asked Jamie.

Max piped up. "You mean it? We're in Adventure?"

"Dude," bellowed Dave, "you were a member after you beat the dog-meat outta yer first ninja."

Jamie thought for a moment. "Okay, Steve and Leslie will wake the students and get them to the elementary gym down the hill." At a curious glance from Dave, he explained, "That gym only has one exit. It'll be easier to defend. They will stay there to guard the students.

"The rest of us will fan out on the school grounds in pairs. Max goes with Pete, Yoshi takes George, Buster gets Jeremy, and Dave and I'll pair off." He looked out the window. Day was beginning to push back the darkness. "We'll regroup at the front steps to this building at 6:30 am."

Buster led a prayer, then the groups began filing out of the room. Jamie grabbed his ninja-to, still in its scabbard, from the front lab table.

Suddenly, a high-pitched ringing sounded through the halls. Jamie ran out of the room to find Steve and Leslie standing next to the fire alarm. "You said to wake the students," explained Leslie with a grin. "You didn't say how."

* * *

Donnie and Tanemura were escorted into a tent. Though the sun was starting to rise, the thick cloud cover that blanketed the sky prevented it from giving much light. And even if the sun were shining on this cold, November morning, the ugly, green canvas that made up the walls and ceiling would have blocked it. The only light sources in their little jail were a small heater and some lanterns that looked as if they could run out of fuel at any time.

Bound to a chair in the center of the tent was a large, bearded man that Don didn't recognize. He wore a checkered skirt and the heater stood in front of him.

"I'm telling you," Dave's dad cried in supreme irritation, "I'm with the Dunklin County Police Academy! We were just fighting the blasted ninja!"

The soldiers ignored them as they seated the new prisoners in chairs on either side of the large man handcuffing their hands behind the backs of the chairs. After they had gone, Donnie asked Tanemura, "What do you suppose they did with the ninja we didn't kill?"

Tanemura shook his head. "One of them mentioned that they were to bring the prisoners who could speak English—us, as it were—to a separate tent. I am not sure where they put the others." The old ninja looked at the incumbent prisoner, who was hunched over, snoring.

"Deck," whispered the old ninja.

"You know this guy?" inquired Donnie.

"He is Jamie and Yoshi's friend," was the response. "He crafted their ninja-tos."

"Why's he wearing a dress?"

Tanemura chuckled. "It is not a dress. It is a kilt."

Deck awoke with a start. "Wh . . . what?" he groaned in confusion. He turned his head and his eyes widened in recognition as they settled on Tanemura. "Hey! What're you doin' here?"

“I might ask you the same question,” returned the jonin.

Deck’s face darkened. “I was on my motorcycle and headin' to the dance. I almost got to the Current River bridge when it blew up. I saw some ninja and went back fer my sword an’ gun. Since the bridge was gone, I swam across at the most shallow part I could find. The good thing is no ninja jumped outta the water to attack me. The bad thing is the army caught me when I got across.”

Don looked at Deck in astonishment. “You swam across a Missouri river . . . in the middle of *November*?”

Deck looked at the other man and replied, “Yeah. So?”

As Dave’s father shook his head in disbelief, Tanemura gave introductions. “Deck, this is Donnie Isaac, Jamie’s uncle. Donnie, this is Deck Pendragon, the greatest weapon-smith in southern Missouri.”

“Probably the *only* weapon-smith in southern Missouri,” corrected Deck.

“True,” chuckled Tanemura.

“How can you be so calm?” demanded Donnie. “My son and nephew are in that school, along with your great-niece and their friends. And we’ve been arrested by the army that’s supposed to be trying to get them out!”

“Faith, Donnie,” returned Tanemura.

* * *

Jamie asked Dave for the time. "Six twenty-seven, dude." They were standing at the front steps, waiting for the other groups to join them. The two of them had seen no sign of the Warui ninja.

As Jamie saw the other groups approaching, a low rumbling sound caught his attention. The sound, which sounded to him like a very loud car that had thrown a rod, grew louder as it approached the school. Now, more familiar sounds joined it. "What is that?" he asked Dave.

"First one sounds like a helicopter," replied the big teen. "And ground vehicles."

As the teams met at the front steps, the first sound reached a deafening pitch as a large, military-style helicopter flew over the high school and across the gravel parking lot, landing on the elementary playground, which was parallel to their building on the eastern side about fifty yards from the front doors of the high school.

As this happened, five black vans drove up the south road, which ran perpendicular to the schoolyard and the playground. They pulled into the parking lot and stopped.

The members of Adventure watched in horrified fascination as black-clad warriors began filing out of the vehicles and gathering on the playground. After a quick count, Buster proclaimed, “Fifty-two.”

Dave gaped. “Dude, even *I* think this is a bit much.”

Without a word, Jeremy grabbed an arrow from his quiver and shot it at the ninja army. It struck one of them in the chest and he dropped. “Fifty-one,” stated the Robin Hood fan.

From the helicopter, a man stepped onto the damp grass as lightning lit the sky and a peal of thunder roared through the small town. He had an air of authority about him that the adolescents couldn’t miss.

“Who is that?” inquired Buster.

“It is the Warui jonin,” responded Yoshi in fearful awe.

Jeremy shot another arrow and took another ninja down. “Fifty,” he said. At sharp glances from Jamie and Buster, he asked defensively, “What? Nobody else is doing anything.” He pulled another arrow, aimed it and fired at the Warui leader. The jonin caught the arrow and snapped it in two.

Jeremy’s mouth fell open. “Well, I wasn’t expecting that.”

The leader of the Warui raised his arm to point in the direction of the teens, yelling something in Japanese. Half of the fifty ninja broke away from the rest and charged toward the school.

"I don't think we need Yoshi to translate that one!" cried Pete.

"Fall back into the school!" ordered Jamie.

They ran through the front doors, pulling them closed. Yoshi quickly locked the doors.

"I've got an idea!" announced Jeremy. "Up the stairs!"

Pete looked at him in disbelief. "What are you . . . nuts?!"

"We'll be trapped up there," said Max.

The Robin Hood fan looked back and forth between Jamie and Yoshi as the first of the ninja arrived and tried to open the locked doors. "Please tell me that one of you has a rope hidden in your suit."

Yoshi replied, "I do."

"Then we won't be trapped!" He lunged up the stairs.

The Warui ninja were starting to cut the thick glass in each of the large windows on either side of the doors. The rest of Adventure followed the Robin Hood fan.

* * *

Obata, the jonin of the Waruiyatsu ninja, watched with contempt as the two Funakoshi chunin fell back into the school with their friends. “Run cowards!” he hissed.

Kenshin, a dragon pendant showing his rank as an attack party leader, stepped forward. “Master,” he began, “what if the *genin* kill the gaijin?”

“Then we will cheer,” was the response, as if it were obvious.

“But Master! Raleigh shamed me during the mission to kill Kuji and Mai Funakoshi! He is supposed to be for me!”

Obata glared at the warrior. “Our victory is more important than your foolish pride!”

* * *

The elementary gym was about half the size of the high school gym, which made the fact that everyone was avoiding John, Freddy and their friends that much more amusing. Steve watched the far side of the gym, where the captain of the basketball team and his sidekicks were sitting by themselves. The rest of the students were crowded on the opposite side. John and his cronies had started to move to the crowded side but, after many colorful insults and death threats, they decided to remain where they were.

Leslie was trying to keep Steve’s attention on a card game they were playing. Everyone was trying to stay in good spirits, though the two members of Adventure wished they could see what was happening to their friends.

Chapter Twenty-Five
Sunday, 6:40 AM

The tent flap opened and a man with the stripes of a colonel entered, followed by two corporals. "Your story checks out," grumbled the colonel, staring at Don. He looked at the two men who had entered with him. "Uncuff'im."

They freed the police teacher, but left the other two in place. "What brings a police academy instructor into an evacuated town?" inquired the commanding officer. "And why were you with one of those ninjas?"

"My son's in the school," replied Donnie, as he rubbed his wrists. "And Tanemura's one of the enemies mentioned on the scroll from Friday night."

"Really?" asked the colonel. "The translator in Jefferson City said there was supposed to be three enemies."

"That would be my great-niece, Yoshika," explained Tanemura, "and my pupil, Jamie Raleigh."

"Jamie's my nephew," said Donnie. "My son and some friends went in with the boy and Yoshi to try and free the students."

"Hey, Peters," rumbled Deck, "if Isaac here vouches for us, can ya let us loose, too?"

Peters motioned for the soldiers to free Deck and Tanemura. Still regarding Don thoughtfully, he asked, "How old is your son?"

"Sixteen," was the response.

"What?! A bunch of kids went in there to fight those ninjas?"

The three former prisoners exchanged glances. "Let's just say they can all take care of themselves," assured Donnie.

* * *

The teens burst into the Home Economics room and slammed the door, locking it. It was the biggest classroom in the school; taking up a third of the top floor. Half of the room was a kitchen with six double-sided sinks, six stoves, two clothes washer-dryer combos and a refrigerator.

Max's voice echoed through the room. "What're we doing here?"

Jeremy ran to the back window, which looked out over the hill on the western side of the building, and opened it. "Give me your rope," he said to Yoshi. After she had handed it over, he secured one end of it to a sewing table that was bolted to the floor. He then threw the other end out the window.

"Everybody climb down," he instructed. "I'll follow in a minute."

“What are you going to do?” asked Jamie suspiciously.

“I’m not going to valiantly give my life, or anything,” chuckled Jeremy. “You need to trust me on that.”

“I hate it when people feel the need to tell me to trust them,” muttered the young ninja.

The teens went down the rope, one at a time, until only Jeremy remained. Running into the kitchen, he lifted the top of the first stove and carefully extinguished the pilot lights. After closing it, he turned on all four burners. He followed suit with the other ranges.

Next, he pulled his shirt collar up to cover his mouth and nose as he ran toward the door, fishing a roll of duct tape, a whetstone and a box of matches out of some of the many pockets that lined his coat . . ..

* * *

Jeremy slid down the rope and landed among his friends at the base of the hill.

“What did you do?” demanded Yoshi.

Noting that all eyes were upon him, he replied, “I slowed them.”

“How?” asked Max.

“You’ll see.”

Buster looked at Jamie. “Why do I have a bad feeling about this?” he asked.

“Probably for the same reason that I do,” was Jamie’s response.

“Guys!” exclaimed Pete, who’d slipped around the southern side of the building to observe the ninja warriors who remained outside. “The others have split up and look like they’re going to come around from both sides!”

“Make a circle,” ordered Jamie. “Don’t let them get behind anyone.” They formed a circle and moved around the southern side of the building . . ..

Chapter Twenty-Six
Sunday, 6:52 AM

"Why haven't you moved on the school?" demanded Donnie.

"I don't have you under arrest anymore," returned Peters, "but I *don't* have to take a lecture on military ethics from a police teacher."

"I'll have you know that I spent twenty years in this man's Air force . . .," argued Dave's father.

"And things have changed a great deal since then," interrupted the colonel. "As long as they have prisoners, the governor's not going to let us go in." He looked at Tanemura. "When we thought you were one of theirs, we figured we might have a bargaining chip. But now . . .."

"You fail to understand how the Warui ninja think," stated the old ninja. "To them, the success of the mission is more important than an individual ninja. Unless you'd captured their leader, they would leave your prisoners to rot, as you Americans say.

"But you do have a bargaining chip with me," Tanemura continued. "The Warui wanted *three* enemies. But they did not get us all. If Jamie, Yoshi and their friends didn't rescue the students, then they are still killing one every hour because we were unable to meet their demands."

"Are you sayin' we should give you to'em?" demanded Deck.

Tanemura's face hardened in resolve. "That is exactly what I am saying."

* * *

Kenji set the heavy glass of the window down next to the doors. He had seen the adolescents run up the stairs. *Cowards and fools*, he thought. Pointing up the hall toward the other set of stairs, he split the group in half and sent each up one set in order to block any escape. He followed the team up the stairs in front of the entrance.

At the top, he looked down the hall to see the other group coming up. There was no sign of the Funakoshi chunin or their friends.

Along one side of the hallway, four doors led to classrooms. Another door on the other side was alone, however.

"Check every room," he ordered in his native tongue.

BANG! The door to the speech room was kicked open and the room was found empty.

BANG! The typing room was empty.

BANG! The computer lab was also empty.

BANG! The high school math room was empty.

The twenty-five ninja converged upon the final door. The team leader smiled beneath his mask. Obata would see that Kenji would be the one to bring the heads of the two Funakoshi chunin. He would get his just rewards.

The team leader pushed impatiently to the front and his foot lunged up to meet the door. His ears caught the *hsssssssss* sound just before he connected. His nose detected the gas an instant before the match that was taped to the bottom of the door scraped along the whetstone, producing fire . . ..

* * *

The eruption of flames shattered the glass in every window of the large room, showering those below with shards. The Warui rounded the corners of the building, ignoring the falling glass as they approached the teens.

A second explosion that thundered through the small town and destroyed the southern wall of the room stopped them in their tracks. Max leaped clear just in time to avoid being crushed by a stove that rode the blast free of the inferno. It struck the ground with a CRASH!

Adventure and the Warui ninja all stared in awe as a screaming ninja stumbled into view, engulfed. He fell from the hole in the wall and hit the ground with a sickening *thud.*

Jamie looked at Jeremy in horror. "What did you do?" he asked weakly.

"I turned off the pilot-lights on the stoves and filled the room with gas. Then, I taped a match to the bottom of the door." He grinned. "Don't know where the last explosion came from. Musta' hit the main gas line."

Jamie looked back up at the gaping hole. Where the stove had stood, a column of fire now steadily torched the ceiling.

"They never had a chance!" raged Buster.

"You think they would have given you one?" countered Jeremy.

The Warui ninja who now surrounded Adventure pulled their swords and attacked.

Jamie's ninja-to and shinobi-to blocked strike after strike. He did his best to disarm his foes, trying to take them down with non-lethal kicks and punches.

Yoshi had quickly earned the respect of the attacking ninja. None of the enemies could touch her through the whirlwind of her twin blades. To her right, George was holding his own. Taking advantage of the longer reach of his weapon, he was able to keep attackers from getting close enough to attack with their swords.

Dave's large fists and feet had been underestimated at the beginning of the fight. But, by the time he had knocked his third opponent cold, he had earned his enemies' respect.

Buster's fast-flying nunchaku formed an impenetrable field around his body. Any of the ninja who got close enough to attack him would invariably move into the path of one of them and get, at the very least, a good-sized headache for his failed attempt.

Pete and Max were taking turns knocking a particular shadow-warrior back and forth in a strange game of "Catch." They would take turns kicking him to each other and continued the game until he finally lost consciousness.

Jeremy shot down his second ninja. Movement in the direction of the playground drew his attention there and he noticed another ninja charging across the schoolyard toward them. He readied another arrow, noting fearfully his dwindling supply, and fired. To his horror, the warrior caught the arrow in mid-flight. "Great," he muttered, "another show-off."

Jamie watched the arrow as it was snatched out of mid-flight, as well. What's more, the young ninja noticed a familiar pendant hanging from the neck of this approaching enemy.

Jamie looked at Yoshi. Her eyes, wide with the remembered terror of a day long past, had obviously seen the warrior. Her gaze moved to her clan brother and they seemed to calm. She reached up and removed her mask, revealing the rest of her beautiful face, her full lips pressed into a line of firm resolve.

Stepping out of her place in the circle, she walked determinedly past Jamie. "He will see the face of the one who will kill him," she declared.

He kicked another ninja in the face as the shadow-warrior blocked his view of Yoshi. When the opponent fell, he saw not only the distance between Yoshi and the approaching ninja growing shorter, but he also noted in shock that the Warui jonin was holding Laura next to the door of the helicopter.

As Jamie watched, the leader of the Funakoshi's rival clan pointed at the cheerleader and then drew his index finger across his throat. The meaning was clear.

After a quick glance to make sure his friends were still doing well, he broke into a run toward the elementary playground.

* * *

As Yoshi approached the evil chunin, his eyes closed and he tossed his head back in hearty laughter. Her eyes narrowed at him. She stood ten feet from him, her twin swords ready, waiting patiently.

He finally stopped laughing, though his voice was still filled with mirth. "Have we not tried this before?"" he cajoled in their native tongue.

"I do not need Jamie to protect me this time," she responded in the same language.

The two enemies circled one another. Yoshi fought to control her rising rage. It didn't help that her opponent looked as if he could start laughing again at any time.

He lunged at her with a downward slash, but she dodged to the left, bringing her right foot out to the side and catching him in the face with it.

He staggered back a few steps. The mask that he wore began to darken with wetness, as it soaked up the blood that was running from his broken nose.

He looked at her in awe, as she declared, "Everything that I am is because of you." She sneered at him. "All of the training, the pain of pushing myself to the limit and *beyond* . . .," she pointed her right ninja-to at him, " . . . it was all to prepare me for this day."

* * *

Jamie approached the Warui jonin warily. The fighting ability of this man was legendary within the Funakoshi clan. And his brutality was infamous. “Let her go,” called the young chunin, over the noise of the helicopter’s engine. “She has nothing to do with this.” He took a deep breath to steady himself. “Let them all go.”

“Jamie!” yelled Laura. “He’s a monster! He killed them all!”

Jamie’s heart fell into his stomach. “Killed who?” he demanded, preparing to lunge at the other ninja if she were to answer that Shawna and Amy were dead.

“The men who brought us to him,” she cried.

Jamie looked at the other ninja in horror. “You . . . you killed your own men?”

“Of course,” replied the jonin, speaking English with practiced ease. "They allowed themselves to be captured. There is no room for weakness in the future of the Waruiyatsu.”

The man stood, unconcerned when Jamie was standing within striking range. “I was expecting the girl to challenge me. According to the prophecy, she is the one to fear.”

Jamie’s eyes narrowed. “What prophecy?”

The jonin did not answer. He merely shoved Laura through the door to the helicopter and pulled his blade . . ..

* * *

Yoshi's blades worked furiously against the ninja-to and shinobi-to of her opponent. His attitude of superiority had fled when he realized he could do nothing but block her attacks.

Several times, she got through his defenses to score minor hits . . . a slash to his shoulder . . . a gash in his right leg. The right side of his mask hung in tatters where she had quickly sliced it in an *X* pattern without breaking his skin. She wanted to prolong his humiliation, not kill him . . . yet.

* * *

Dave lifted the last of the Warui over his head, spun around three times, then dropped him on top of one of the unconscious shadow-warriors. The dizzy ninja tried to rise, but was knocked cold by one of Buster's well-placed kicks to the face.

The big teen, a look of exaggerated irritation on his face, chided, "I wasn't done with him, yet!"

Buster placed his hand over a small cut on his left forearm and looked at his friend in disapproval. "You're enjoying this too much."

Dave patted him on the back, nearly knocking him from his feet. "Lighten up, dude.

Always enjoy every fight like it could be the last one you'll ever be in."

"I hope it *is*," responded Buster.

Dave looked around at his friends, all bruised and battered, but still alive. "I guess its over," he sighed in mock depression.

"Yoshi's still fighting," Max commented.

When Buster and Dave looked at her opponent, their jaws dropped.

"He's the guy who led the team that killed her parents!" exclaimed Buster, who broke into a run toward the duel. "We've got to stop this!"

"She's a lot better fighter than before," said Pete.

"Exactly!" Buster yelled back without slowing. "She'll butcher him!"

* * *

Jamie was hard-pressed to block his opponent's attacks. The jonin made the chunin who killed Yoshi's father seem like a neophyte.

"Are you nervous, gai-jin?" asked his enemy. "Will you tell me how it feels to have your entrails cast upon the ground and fed upon by the vultures?"

The sound of metal striking metal rang out, each strike hurting the young ninja's teeth. His bones shook with every connection of the blades. How could this small man be so strong?

Shawna's face appeared in the open door of the helicopter, only to be pulled roughly back by another ninja. At least he knew she was alive.

Unfortunately, he had made the mistake of taking his eyes off his opponent. A quick swipe of the jonin's sword had Jamie's own ninja-to laying on the ground several feet away.

The young chunin dodged a swing at his neck, though the blade bit into his left shoulder. He gasped as a bolt of pain shot down his arm. He wasn't fast enough to avoid having his feet swept from underneath him. Landing painfully on his back, he looked up, panic stricken, at his opponent, who seemed to smile under his mask as he shoved the tip of his sword toward the teen's face.

Jamie's hands shot up, clapping together with the blade pressed flat between them, his fingers intertwining to lock it in place. Now, it was a push-of-war. And, as the pointed tip edged closer to his face, he realized he was losing . . ..

* * *

Yoshi spin-kicked her opponent in the face. He stumbled back a few steps, so she pressed her attack by punching him in the face, her blow augmented by the hilt of her sword.

He gasped in pain as this attack struck his broken nose.

As the male warrior struggled to maintain his balance, she kicked his ninja-to from his hand and, in the same spinning motion, swept his legs from under him. As his back slammed into the ground, the shinobi-to was wrenched from his grasp.

The kunoichi crossed her blades over the terrified assassin's throat. "Is it not amazing," she began in her native language, visions of this man standing over her father's fallen body filling her mind, "how villains always seem to create their own worst enemies?" She clamped the blades closer to his throat, taking surprisingly little comfort at the fear in his pleading eyes.

"Yoshi," came a gentle, familiar voice. "Don't." And then Buster was standing next to her, followed by Dave.

"My father was a great warrior," spoke Yoshi. "They could never have defeated him without me as his weakness." Tears started building in her eyes. "And the cowards never even let my mother know what hit her." She squeezed the blades tighter. The cloth around his throat darkened. She was breaking the skin. As the tears overflowed, she was barely able to whisper, "He deserves to die."

Buster stood behind her and gently placed his hands over hers. "Only God can make that call," he told her. "This man will be tried by God, just like all of us." He firmly pulled her arms back.

"What do you want Him to see when you stand before Him and He looks back on today?"

She shivered as the tears flowed freely. "I could not help them." Her swords fell from numb hands and Buster embraced her as she sobbed into his shoulder. *"I could not help them . . .."*

The male chunin sighed in relief and started to rise, but was halted when a large, army boot-clad foot came down on his chest, holding him in place. Dave muttered, "Just because she ain't gonna make hamburger outta ya, don't mean ya get t'leave, dude."

* * *

The tip of the blade was barely an inch from his nose. Theoretically, the way he was holding the blade was supposed to keep him from being cut. However, the sharp pain in his left hand, as well as the thin trickle of blood that ran out between his thumb and index finger, made him realize that it wasn't working. The Warui jonin was leaning into the sword and Jamie barely had the leverage to hold the blade at bay, especially considering his wounded shoulder.

A drip of water fell from the sky and struck his brow. It was beginning to rain.

Who am I kidding? thought the young ninja, as the blade touched his nose. *I can't keep this up.*

In desperation, he jerked to the right and released his grip, letting the jonin's weight drive the sword into the ground next to the prone young man's head. The enemy gasped in surprise as the young ninja lashed out with his right foot to trip the Warui leader, who was suddenly on the ground next to Jamie, his head beside Jamie's foot.

The young man kicked the older man across the face, then leaped to his feet. As the jonin followed suit, Jamie slammed his right fist into his face. Continuing the momentum, he spun around and brought the heel of his left foot across the shadow-warrior's head. The man was knocked backward into the side of the helicopter and slid to the ground, unconscious.

The clouds that had been blanketing the sky for days started to open up in full force. In seconds, Jamie and his senseless enemy were drenched.

Then the helicopter started to lift off.

Jamie charged forward and leaped through the open door. He could see another ninja in here. The girls were here, too. They were bound on a bench that was next to the door in which he'd come. Though visibly shaken, they looked unharmed.

Shawna yelled, "Jamie look out!"

He ducked in time to avoid being hit by a sword wielded by a warrior who had been hidden next to the door. The young ninja grabbed his attacker in irritation and threw him out of the helicoptor. He fell fifteen feet and hit the ground below.

Another enemy charged him, but flew out of the helicopter when Jamie simply stepped aside.

Looking back out the door, he nearly fainted. They had risen up at least sixty feet in a matter of seconds. His friends below, who were busy binding the jonin and one of the men who had just fallen from the vehicle, looked like ants. He had little hope that the last ninja had survived the fall.

"What?" demanded Shawna.

He gulped. "I'm an acrophobic."

"What?" asked Amy.

"He's scared of heights," explained Shawna.

Amy chuckled, until she realized that they weren't kidding. "Oh, *you're* in the right place."

He pulled a knife from his boot and cut Shawna loose. Giving the weapon to her, he instructed, "Use this to get them loose. I'm going to see if I can persuade the pilot to turn around."

Shawna went to work on their ropes while Jamie stepped into the cockpit. A single ninja sat at the controls. Jamie didn't have a chance to say a word before the man's dagger was in hand and he was lunging toward Jamie, who caught his wrist and shoved him back into the control panel. The teen grimaced as his wounded shoulder hit the back of the pilot's seat in the cramped compartment.

"You idiot!" grunted the young hero. "You've got to get back to the controls! You'll kill us all!"

The man yelled something in Japanese.

"Great," groaned Jamie, as he slammed the back of the other man's wrist into his knee, disarming him, "you can't understand a word I'm saying, can you?"

Jamie slammed his elbow into the ninja's face, watching him slide to the floor, unconscious. He dropped into the pilot's seat and grabbed the controls.

"What happened?" asked Shawna.

The young ninja risked a look back and saw Laura and Amy looking out the side door of the helicoptor.

"I knocked him out," he responded in frustration. He had to yell to be heard.

"Oh," responded Shawna as she sat in the co-pilot's seat. "You don't sound pleased."

"Let's just say that flying a helicopter wasn't in my training."

She looked at the control stick. "You move us with that thing." She pointed. "It's called a *cyclic*."

He looked at her hopefully. "You know about helicopters?"

She shook her head. "Only from what I saw in *Airwolf*."

He sighed. “I’m going to try to land.”

He moved the cyclic and the copter lurched around and headed toward the elementary building.

“You’re doing well,” commented Shawna. “Take it down slow.”

Jamie pulled over the elementary building. “How far up are we?” he yelled back.

Amy answered him. “About ten feet above the roof!”

“Jump!” He looked back at them. “I can’t land. And I don’t know how long I can keep it steady! JUMP!”

Amy took Laura’s hand and pulled them out of the door. They landed safely on the roof.

Jamie looked at Shawna. “You, too.”

She shook her head, her eyes filling with tears. “I can’t just leave you here.”

He thought for a moment. “I saw a parachute when I jumped in. It’s on the back wall. Bring it to me.”

She jumped up and ran into the passenger area, returning a moment later with the green pack.

“Now hold the control steady while I put it on,” he said. She grabbed the cyclic and he stood, donning the pack and fastening it in place.

He sat in the pilot's seat again and said, "After you jump, I'll take it up high enough for me to parachute out."

"I thought you were scared of heights?" she demanded.

"I'm more scared of seeing you die," he explained with a smile.

She leaned over and kissed him, then ran back to the door. He watched as she jumped to the roof of the elementary building. Then he pulled back on the control and his heart began to pound in his chest as the vehicle ascended.

A flash of metal in his field of vision alerted him to the fact that the pilot was conscious again. Jamie caught the ninja's wrist, the blade of the Warui's dagger mere inches from the teen's nose.

In desperation, the young ninja pulled back on the cyclic as hard as he could, knocking the other ninja off balance. Jamie's right fist connected squarely with the ninja's jaw, sending him reeling back into the passengers' area.

Jamie leveled out just as a flash of lighting lit the sky and struck one of the chopper blades, breaking it off. Jamie grabbed the control and pulled, but it was frozen.

He leaped to his feet and ran from the cockpit, grabbing the unconscious pilot and looking out the door. He was at least two hundred feet up and the copter had turned to begin a descent back toward the elementary school building.

He held the ninja in a bear hug, closed his eyes, muttered a quick prayer and leaped.

Holding the other ninja as best he could with his left arm, Jamie grabbed the ripcord and pulled, releasing the parachute. The resulting jerk as it caught the wind nearly caused him to drop the Warui. Turning to look at the copter, Jamie's eyes followed it as it flew over the elementary building and toward the Baptist church.

I can't look! He closed his eyes tightly, turning his head away from the inevitable crash. The wind blew through his hair, its breath muffling the other noises around him. The crash broke through the loud whispering with an explosion that made Jeremy's destruction of the Home Ec room pale in comparison.

The explosion roused the Warui warrior. He groaned as he looked down, seeing the ground moving up to meet them. As they were only about twenty feet up, Jamie released him. Screaming what Jamie could only guess was a Japanese swear word, the ninja dropped to the ground in the midst of Adventure.

Then Jamie looked toward the crash site. There wasn't a mark on the church. But the abortion clinic was in ruins.

The young ninja landed in a run. As he slowed his momentum, he dropped to the ground and kissed it.

Dave and Buster had helped the girls down from the roof of the one-story elementary building.

Shawna ran up to him and leaped into his arms. He allowed himself a moment of peace as he kissed her.

"Brother, you are hurt," came Yoshi's voice from behind him.

Jamie sat Shawna down and turned to look at his clan-sister. "It's nothing a few stitches and a week's worth of sleep won't fix." He looked past her and noticed the Warui ninja who had been dueling with her , sitting on the ground. He was bound, but alive. "I'm proud of you, sis."

The sound of approaching land vehicles caught everyone's attention. "Not again!" exclaimed Max.

An army truck came into view on the road that ran along the south side of the school. Two more followed it. As the teens watched, not quite knowing what to make of this turn of events, the vehicles turned up the east road and drove toward them.

The front vehicle pulled onto the elementary playground and drove forward until it was barely twenty feet away. Then the doors opened and two men in army camouflage climbed out.

But what caught the most attention were three of the people who climbed out of the back of the truck.

"Dad!" exclaimed Dave.

"Uncle!" exploded Yoshi.

"Deck?" asked Jeremy.

The three walked up to them and Donnie embraced Dave. "Are you okay, son?"

"I'm fine, dad." He chuckled. "Kickin' ninja butt made this a pretty enjoyable weekend!"

Tanemura put one hand on each of his students' shoulders. "I knew that you would be okay."

Jamie and Yoshi swelled with pride and then hugged each other. They chuckled when they heard Dave demand, "Hey! Who's the dude in the dress?"

They laughed out loud when they heard Deck reply defensively, "It's not a *dress*, it's a KILT!"

Epilogue
Sunday, 4:00 PM

Ouch, thought Jamie, *this cot sure is uncomfortable.* The young ninja was lying inside the ugly, green medical tent in the army encampment. The sound of various army vehicles moving outside filled his ears, covering the more peaceful sound of the river, which was actually thirty or so feet away.

Reaching down beside the cot, he picked the vest of his ninja suit up from the floor and examined it. "I think I know what Yoshi'll be giving me for Christmas," he muttered to himself.

The flap opened and Yoshi stepped in. "How are you feeling, brother?" she asked.

"My shoulder still hurts. But at least not as bad as earlier." He shrugged his good shoulder. "I guess the stuff they gave me to numb it is starting to kick in. Just not as fast as I'd like. My hand still hurts, too."

Yoshi walked up to the cot and kneeled down beside it. Looking at the vest, she declared, "I think that you will need a new suit for Christmas."

Jamie chuckled.

She laid her head on his chest and whispered, "I really did fear that we would lose you today."

He put his good arm around her and said, "God was with us."

The sound of someone nervously clearing her throat caught their attention. Shawna had just entered the tent.

Yoshi climbed hastily to her feet. "This is your place now," she said to Shawna while pointing at her clan brother.

To Jamie, the sound of her voice was different. "Is something wrong?"

"No," was the kunoichi's reply. "I will leave you two alone."

She quickly exited the tent. Shawna moved over and took Yoshi's spot. He wrapped his good arm around the girl as she stated, "She's jealous."

"What?" asked Jamie incredulously. "No. We don't like each other like that."

She looked up into his eyes. "Girls can tell these things."

Jamie was about to respond, when the tent flap opened again and Tanemura stepped in. Jamie's ninja master smiled as he approached the young couple.

"If I weren't in so much pain, I'd bow to you, Master," said Jamie.

"Do not worry about that, Jamie," replied Tanemura. "I am just happy that you are safe, considering the fact that you defeated the leader of the Warui ninja in combat."

Jamie looked seriously at his teacher. “Master Tanemura, when I was fighting the Warui jonin, he mentioned a prophecy. He said Yoshi was the one that they were supposed to fear.”

“I believe that I can explain that,” was the response. “In the seventeenth century, Christianity was still relatively new in Japan, which had begun to open its borders for trade with the west. Despite the good nature of the Portuguese traders who visited our country, Japanese followers of Christ were often persecuted. This persecution led to an uprising called the Shimabara Rebellion. One of the leaders of this uprising was an adolescent named Amakusa Shirō. Many of his followers attributed special powers to him. Apparently this young man had the Christian gift of prophecy and actually predicted, to both of our clans, the end of our war at the end of the second millennium of the Lord. He said that the last of the Warui leaders would fall to a female of our clan, unless they made peace with us. When Yoshi was born, her father felt that she would be the one.”

“What happened to the rebellion?” asked Jamie.

Tanemura clasped his hands behind his back. “The rebels were all killed during a siege at a castle in the Hizen Provence. They were slaughtered, to the man, for their faith.” He sighed. “Many of the Funakoshi were involved in the battle on the side of the Shogun.”

"Ouch," groaned Jamie. "There's a stain on the history of our clan."

"The Dutch, in order to gain the trust of the Japanese government, bombarded the castle, as well."

"What do you think?" Shawna asked Tanemura. "I mean, about the prophecy?"

"I am more disposed to believe it because he did not simply pick out the clan that was aligned against his people." He shook his head. "Despite the ways of the Waruiyatsu, they chose to remain neutral in the uprising."

Again, the tent flap opened, and Deck stuck his head in. "Uh, Jamie," he spoke, "there's a photographer here from the Doniphan newspaper. He wants to get a picture of Adventure."

"Why?" inquired Jamie as he climbed to his feet, wincing the whole time.

"Well," responded Deck, "in just the last couple o' hours, all the newspapers in Missouri have started calling you guys heroes."

"How dumb," remarked Jamie as he put his good arm around Shawna's shoulders and the two walked out the flap.

They were escorted to a clearing, where a man Jamie didn't recognize was standing with Dave, Buster and the others.

"Any word on when we're supposed to get to go home?" Jamie heard Max ask Steve.

“They said they’d have make-shift bridges ready by Tuesday, so everyone who actually lives inside the city limits can come home,” was his brother’s response.

Dave, Buster, Yoshi, George, Jeremy, Steve, Leslie, Max and Pete had already lined up for the picture. Jamie reluctantly pulled away from Shawna and took his place next to Dave and Buster.

“All right,” instructed the photographer as he put the camera up to his face, “say *cheese*!”

At the POP of the flash, the name of every kind of cheese imaginable, from Swiss to head-cheese, was yelled.

After the picture, a man stepped up to the group and said, “I’m Del King, from *96.9*. I was hoping to get an interview.”

“Hi, Del,” greeted Shawna.

“Shawna Weston,” began the reporter, “I didn’t know you were here!”

“You two know each other?” asked Jamie.

“He goes to my church,” explained Shawna. “How’d you get across the river?”

“The military brought some of the press across in boats.”

The middle-aged reporter looked at the male chunin and said, “Now, you’re Jamie Raleigh?”

Jamie nodded.

"And you're the leader of . . . of . . .," he looked at his notepad, "oh, what was the name of your group?"

Jamie grinned as he looked around at the other members of his club.

In unison, the adolescents all exclaimed, "ADVENTURE!!!"

END

Also available
From Jeffrey Allen Davis
and GCD Publishing

Lily's Redemption

A Christian mystery thriller exploring the dangerous effects of pornography, it is available in paperback, Kindle and Nook editions.

Coming Soon

Klandestine Maneuvers

An update to Jeffrey Allen Davis's second book, Klandestine Maneuvers sees the members of *Adventure*, along with some new faces, facing an influx of racists who have come to Sera to terrorize the town's only black family, the Robertsons.